ODDS AGAINST TOMORROW

ODDS AGAINST TOMORROW

J.S. TRENT

Edited by Maddie Senator of Eschler Editing
Cover design by Paramita Creative
Book design by Maureen Cutajar (www.gopublished.com)

Library of Congress Control Number: 1-5717084261

ISBN: (E-book) 978-0-9993208-1-5 | (Paperback): 978-0-9993208-0-8 | (Hardcover): 978-0-9993208-2-2

For Ryan Nutter and Krystle LaJaune

CONTENTS

CHAPTER ONE

Blood and Promises

Lordsburg, 1884

A deputy marshal strode along with his Winchester carried casually at his side. He was making the morning rounds. He paused briefly and peered down a back alley. Apparently seeing something, he moved into the dim area. It was early, and the rising sun had not yet chased away the darkened shadows lingering from the night before. In one such spot behind a saloon, the deputy approached a man lying curled up on the ground. He coaxed him with the tip of his boot. "Come on," he said. "Last night's worn off. You can look forward to your hangover keeping you company today—that gift you find at the bottom of every whiskey bottle."

The man rolled over and mumbled in response, its meaning impenetrable, his words directed at either the deputy or someone in his dream.

The deputy persisted. "Go home to your wife, Tom," he added with seriousness as he moved on.

1

Not far off he came upon two sleeping men who had found similar sanctuary. They were facing each other and their snores alternated as if in response to each other, giving the appearance that they were in deep discussion of the matters that day.

Apparently amused, the deputy looked at them and scrutinized the state they were in. "Let's break up the board meetin' and move on," he said finally.

One of the men stirred. "Leave us alone, Charlie," he managed to say, then got comfortable again and went quickly went back to his previous condition.

Charlie shook his head with disapproval. "Ready to set the world on fire, aren't ya?" he asked, not expecting a response. "Like two cougars ready to leap into the fray." He then lifted his eyes from the two men and stepped away, continuing through the back alley. He approached and nodded to a merchant, who was going about his daily routine and preparing to open up for business. The merchant smiled in return and then retreated inside his backdoor marked Stimson's Feed & Grain.

The deputy moved along, nearing the end of the alleyway. There was movement behind him. Alerted at the last moment, he was too late to react. A figure stepped from one of the still-darkened shadows with a bowie knife and thrust the blade into his back.

Moments later, the killer emerged from the back alley into the bright morning light. He now carried the deputy's Winchester. He paused briefly to look about as if to see if he'd been noticed. Satisfied, he glanced to the rising sun and moved toward his horse tied nearby. He quickly whirled to the sound of a fast approaching snarling dog—the unmistakable pounding of a large four-footed animal gathering traction in the dirt. He cocked the Winchester and brought it to bear on a black mouth cur. The yellow dog stopped within a few feet and began barking loudly at the stranger.

———◆———

On another street, Marshal Matthew Donovan strode along with a youthful step, his eyes set ahead. The yellow cur's barking in the background disturbed the quiet of the morning of a day just getting started. With evident satisfaction, his eyes scanned the people and the structures of this town, recently founded on the newly laid tracks of the Southern Pacific. The railroad missed the nearby town of Shakespeare by three miles. The bell now tolled for that community. And like fleas jumping from a dying dog, businesses began to move to the new and growing railroad town of Lordsburg, and with it Shakespeare began to move toward ghost town.

Matthew's step this morning was that of a man with a purpose. All about his manner were the indications that his destination this day was a happy one. He observed the townspeople starting to fill the streets and go about their business under the empty blue sky. Most were dressed to keep out the early morning chill of this first day of November.

Matthew smiled and tipped his Stetson in response to casual greetings. He was now at twenty-eight years of age, and it had been a full year since he was offered the marshal position. He had already been assistant marshal of Wilcox in the Arizona Territory and in Tucson, where he'd made a name for himself with his unflinching courage and dedication. It was also where he'd met his wife, Rachel. Matthew had accepted the position of marshal in Lordsburg and moved with his new bride to live on a horse ranch just outside of town. She was in Lordsburg this morning. He was on his way to meet her—she was his destination.

———◆———

As the killer faced the cur, he quickly looked about to see what attention the barking was garnering. Returning his eyes to the agitated dog, he backed toward his horse with the barrel leveled at the well-muscled animal. As he neared, the now-stirred up horse pulled at its tether and lifted its head, showing the whites of its eyes. He untethered it, and with his rifle still aimed at the barking cur, he attempted to mount. The horse reared and stepped away from him, pawing and stamping the ground. Finally getting the animal under control, the killer got a foot in the stirrup and swung up into the saddle. He sheathed the Winchester in the scabbard, turned the reins and the horse quickly stepped away—the yellow dog not letting up.

Matthew moved down the boardwalk. His gaze moved to two elderly men who were sitting on a bench outside of a merchant's store he was approaching. They were in a heated debate over the candidates Cleveland and Blaine in the 1884 presidential election just days away on November 4. Though New Mexico's territory status would not allow them to vote, the men's discussion was just as agitated as the dog barking in the distance. Their words just as fevered over the Democrat and Republican as if the two arguing men were allowed to cast a ballot, and each were absolutely determined to convince the other of the error in his thinking.

Up ahead, Rachel emerged from a merchant's store into the morning light—and Matthew's path—unaware of his approach. She was a handsome woman with green eyes and dark brown hair, and was four years his junior. She adjusted her bagged purchases in her arms just as his two strong arms wrapped themselves around her from behind. Angling a look, she said, warmly, "I was hoping to see you this morning."

"A wife buying presents for her husband?" Matthew asked.

She smiled. "Well, if you'd be happy with coffee, bread, and two candles—yes."

"At least the candles sound romantic," he responded, and then he spun her around.

"We'll light them tonight," she said. "I promise."

Matthew brought Rachel to him and kissed her. He then

5

let his eyes rest on her for a long moment. "God you are beautiful. I'm a lucky man."

"I'll see you tonight," she said, and stepped away.

Matthew's eyes lingered on her as she moved down the boardwalk. He then turned his attention to the other side of the street. Before stepping off the boardwalk, he glanced to the rising hard sun.

The yellow cur stopped barking in the distance.

Matthew stepped off and strode into the street.

"Hey, lawman," came the casual, confident challenge.

Matthew turned his eyes to the voice. In his sight were three stark figures facing him in the short distance, silhouetted against the morning sun. One stood prominently a few steps in front of the others, with a relaxed and readied hand near his holster. The two other men stood at each side and a few feet behind him.

Rachel paused on the walkway. She looked back over her shoulder to her husband and to the man calling ominously to him. From the shaded boardwalk, she could see that the man had a hardened exterior and a confident grin. The two other men with him were of the same measure. She watched as all business and social interaction in the street and on the boardwalk ceased. To her, it was if time had stopped.

Matthew turned fully to face the silhouetted men.

"De La Rosa," he said, identifying the man calling to him.

Rachel watched as all those on the street hurried onto the boardwalk on each side of the street, some gathering near her.

With her thoughts and eyes on her husband and the men calling to him, she pushed past those standing close by, not seeing their faces, and began moving back down the walkway toward Matthew. She heard a few people call her name. She passed those hastily moving away, and colliding and jostling with those not looking where they were going. She hardly noticed her purchases being knocked from her grip, spilling onto the planks beneath her feet.

De La Rosa's grin widened. He swiftly drew his gun and fired twice. The two gunshots hit Matthew before he could clear leather, hurling him backwards and impacting the earth hard.

"No!" Rachel cried out from deep within her soul. She hurried into the street and toward her wounded husband.

Matthew struggled. He attempted to rise and bring his gun to bear. He pulled back the trigger on his Colt single-action army revolver. The barrel flash of the outlaw's gun in the distance came an instant later, the bullet passing through Matthew and kicking up dust behind him. He was thrown back to the ground. His struggle ceased.

Rachel reached her husband and cradled him. Ignoring everything around her, she gazed down into the eyes of her now-dying husband.

Nearby, Hannah Bristow, a bystander on the boardwalk, stepped out onto the street. Obviously grieved at what had taken place, she looked to the outlaw down the street. "I saw it," she called out. "You didn't give him a chance."

Smiling broadly, De La Rosa moved the gun barrel sights to her. His accomplices swiftly drew their guns on the gathering, murmuring crowd.

Hannah's husband, Mayor Uriah Bristow, stepped out of the crowd and into the street. He cautiously moved to his wife, took hold of her arm, and pulled her back to the boardwalk out of harm's way.

De La Rosa holstered his gun. "Hey, lawman," he called out, "You should have minded your own business."

Matthew's eyes peered up into Rachel's. His words fading, "Rachel . . . I . . ."

"I love you, Matthew," she said, with tears welling up. She watched him close his eyes and take his last breath. After a moment, she lifted her gaze to the silhouetted figure of the man down the street who had just taken her husband's life. She squinted and shaded her eyes. The face she'd seen from the boardwalk was now lost to the sun. Rachel quickly reached for her husband's gun that lay nearby. De La Rosa quickly drew his gun again and fired, the bullet hitting near the Colt, kicking up dirt. Rachel recoiled, and then moved toward it once again.

"Rachel!" Hannah cried out from the boardwalk, alarmed.

Rachel paused, her eyes still on the man down the street.

Uriah Bristow let go of his wife's arm and motioned for her not to move. He swallowed hard, and with his eyes on the killers down the street, he cautiously stepped off into the sun once again, and moved toward Rachel. He kicked the gun away from her reach.

De La Rosa laughed. "Come on, my friends, let's go." Then he added in a dismissive tone, "It is only his woman." The outlaws' eyes swept the boardwalks, looking for a possible threat. Evidently realizing that there was no danger from the other men that had gathered, De La Rosa and the other two holstered their guns and moved to mount their horses that were tied off nearby. He swung up into the saddle and turned his gaze to Rachel once more. She had not taken her eyes off him. His smile faded. He turned his horse, and the three men spurred their horses out of town. At the outskirts, they were joined on horseback by the man who now carried the deputy's Winchester in his saddle scabbard.

Rachel observed the four men ride way. Her eyes moved back to her dead husband for a few final moments.

A man hurried up to Uriah Bristow on the boardwalk. "Mayor, the deputy's dead, too," he announced excitedly.

"Charlie?" he responded. "Damn."

The man nodded. "Yes sir, in the alley near Stimson's Feed and Grain—slit open with a knife. A big one from the looks of it," he added. "I saw him when I went to find my dog. I heard him barkin'."

"Did you see anything?"

"No, but Mr. Stimson believes he saw the man that did it."

"Bring him here, will you?"

"Yes, sir, right away." He then noticed Rachel observing

him and tipped his hat to her. "My condolences, ma'am," he said, before hurrying off the way he had come.

"Mr. Bristow, could you assist me?" Rachel asked.

"Of course," he responded, quickly, apparently embarrassed he hadn't done so already. He looked to a few men on the boardwalk. "John—Matt," he said, waving them over.

The two men acknowledged the request and stepped off the boardwalk toward Rachel.

She had moved her eyes back to her husband. She could see the men's boots as they moved in, positioning themselves to lift Matthew. After a moment, they knelt and gently took hold of him. She released him. They took a firmer grip and carefully lifted her husband from her lap and moved away.

"They'll see to him, Rachel," said Mr. Bristow.

Rachel rose to her feet—her gaze vacant. Those on the boardwalk watched her in silence. She gathered her emotions and took a deliberate breath. She brushed the hair from her face, then her eyes settled on the telegraph office down the street.

"We're . . . terribly sorry," Mr. Bristow offered. With a pained expression, he added, "And I'm sorry we couldn't find it within us to help your—"

Before he could finish, Rachel moved purposefully toward the telegraph office.

Mr. Bristow peered after her.

Inside the telegraph office, the young wide-eyed clerk was looking out the window, watching the events unfold. He saw

Rachel move down the street in his direction. Not comprehending her destination, he simply observed her. As she grew nearer, it suddenly came upon him that his enterprise was her destination. He came to attention real quick and immediately returned to his desk. He looked up when she entered with purpose. Speechless, his mouth agape, he beheld her as she stepped over to him.

"I want to dispatch a message to my father, Mr. Hamilton Pierce, in Tucson, immediately."

"Yes, yes, of course, Mrs. Donovan." He quickly gathered pencil and paper.

She dictated, "Matthew murdered. Come at once. Will pursue. Signed, Rachel."

The young man finished scribbling her message. "Yes, I have it, Mrs. Donovan." He extended it for her to confirm.

She took it in hand and read. She nodded, and gave it back to him. "Please send it right away." She pushed money toward the clerk and moved to leave.

"Yes, Mrs. Donovan."

The clerk's eyes followed her out the door. He stepped over to the telegraph machine and took a seat. He looked to the paper in his hand and saw that it was now stained with Matthew's blood. He peered at it momentarily, then lifted his eyes to the window beyond which Rachel was passing out of view. He took a deliberated breath, lowered his gaze to the message once again, and began to tap dots and dashes on the telegraph key.

11

CHAPTER TWO

Out of the Past

Two hours later on the Pierce Ranch in the foothills of the Santa Catalina Mountains just north of Tucson in the Arizona Territory, Hamilton Pierce conducted his buckboard. He was a man of forty-three years who had an easy smile and a commanding countenance. His face was etched from an active life in the sun. They were the markings of a life well-lived. Hamilton looked about at the ranch he had built from scratch and to the cattle and horses that now filled it. It had become a daily routine for him to get out onto the land and he enjoyed it. All about him was the fall foliage on vivid display in the crisp air. Among the many trees were the maples in their various tones of rust and red, and the aspens with their yellow-gold leaves. Hamilton liked how the changing seasons painted different landscapes on his land.

Ever present on these outings was Elihu Merritt, who was riding horseback to the rear of the buckboard. He was lean as a sapling and broad-shouldered, and at twenty-five he was already ranch foreman. He followed dutifully behind Hamilton as he had done countless times. He was a stray from an unhappy upbringing who had shown up at the Pierce Ranch looking for work eight years ago. He took every chance to ride with Hamilton and learn from the man he admired, and he wanted to be available to carry out his next directive with all alacrity. Elihu was also there to give protection, though it was not asked of him. Riding abreast of Elihu this day was one of the ranch hands.

Hamilton pulled the reins on the buckboard and came to a stop. His eyes swept the land. His gaze soon settled on a cattle herd grazing nearby. He then lifted his eyes to the morning sky.

"It's a fine day, Elihu—a fine day," he said with great satisfaction.

He was a man who had begun to appreciate the days, not because of his age, but because of the gathering accumulation of days behind him when his life seemed forfeit to the dangerous circumstances he found himself in. He would often think back on those early days. Back before such things meant anything to him, back when days came and went without much notice for there were so many in front of him.

"Yes sir, it is," Elihu responded.

There was a sudden rush through the trees close to Hamilton. He looked up to see the branches and leaves yielding to the hurried breeze. He took stock of the same cold brushing by him. "But these days are far spent. The wind has become bitter."

Elihu and the ranch hand turned to a fast-approaching rider in the distance.

"Rider coming in," announced the ranch hand. "Quick," he added for emphasis.

Elihu rose up in his saddle for better advantage. "Looks like Jess."

Hamilton turned his eyes and thoughts to the ranch hand coming hard.

Jess Whitt galloped in and pulled reins. He was the same age as Elihu and the two had become good friends.

Hamilton took in the urgency of his approach and demeanor and peered at him questioningly.

"The marshal from Tucson delivered a message to the house," Jess said, the words spilling over one another. "Mrs. Pierce says come quick."

Hamilton cracked the horsewhip and the buckboard lurched forward. He knew his wife, Julia, was not prone to urgency. He last heard this tone when they lost their son years ago. His large ranch house looked small in the distance—a distance he was trying to shorten real quick. There was another sharp crack of the whip. "Yah!" he yelled.

"What is it, Jess?" asked Elihu.

"She wouldn't say."

They spurred their horses to catch up to Hamilton.

15

———•———

The main house drew near. Hamilton's buckboard hurriedly approached the gated entrance. He quickly passed underneath the wrought-iron that stretched across overhead proclaiming the Pierce Ranch. Close behind, Elihu, Jess, and the ranch hand followed him through.

Hamilton slowed the horse to a trot as he moved up the well-worn, tree-lined route toward the main house. It was a large two-story with a wraparound porch befitting a successful rancher. There was much activity around the grounds today. Children from the ranch hands' families often played together, which was a happy and common sight on his property. They interrupted their games and dashed up to greet Hamilton as he approached. He pulled reins and halted. The winded horse snorted, its head and neck bobbing up and down as it took in air.

"Mr. Pierce! Mr. Pierce!" the smiling children cried out, each hoping to get his attention.

Hamilton took in his enthusiastic welcome and stepped down from the buckboard. He knew the children were unaware of the urgency of his return. He looked to Elihu and motioned to the buckboard. "Take care of it, will ya, Elihu?"

"Yes sir, Mr. Pierce." With all alacrity, Elihu spurred forward, grasped the rein and lead the horse and buckboard away.

The children gathered around Hamilton. He hoisted one child, patted the head of another, and spoke to all. "You are as beautiful as this November morning."

"Will you take us on a buggy ride?" one asked.

"I couldn't imagine a greater way to spend the day," Hamilton responded. He then turned to Julia, who was on the porch waiting. She carried a concerned posture and countenance—a look he had come to recognize. Momentarily returning her gaze, Hamilton returned to the eager and bright faces before him. He set the child down. "But let's make it another time." Seeing that he had disappointed them, he added as consolation, "We'll picnic by the lake." The children eagerly agreed. "Now run along and don't forget." They darted away, returning to their activities. Hamilton, once again, turned his gaze to Julia.

He moved up the steps of the porch. His wife stood at the top. He stopped two steps before her, placing a foot on the next step, and peered at her.

Her gaze unwavering, Julia extended to him Rachel's telegram. "Matthew's dead. Killed in Lordsburg."

Hamilton ignored the telegram, searching his wife's face for what was most important to both of them.

"Rachel is fine," she informed him, reading his unspoken question. "The telegram is from her."

Hamilton took the message in hand, moved up the last few steps, and read. Pained, he leaned against a post, staring at the ground, and then lifted his eyes to regard the splendid morning he had just been enjoying. His gaze moved to the children playing in the distance.

"The marshal said they're violent men of the worst kind," Julia stated. "The one who shot Matthew goes by the name Juan de La Rosa; the others he's not sure of. All horse thieves, heading east." She stepped closer. "Rachel spoke of pursuing these men."

"And we will," Hamilton responded, hoping she didn't read into Rachel's words what he had.

"We *both* know what she is going to do," Julia came back. "She means she won't wait for you."

Hamilton took a deliberate breath, and nodded in thought. "She'll wait until after the funeral and leave in the morning," he said finally. "We'll have that much time. A day—no more."

Julia stepped away and settled on the porch swing, peering out over the ranch.

Hamilton returned his gaze to the telegram in his hand, and then lifted his eyes to the distance once again. After a moment, he sighed as if giving way to an inward struggle and coming to a hard decision. "Elihu!" he called out.

Elihu spurred his horse and galloped over. "Yes sir, Mr. Pierce?"

"Matthew Donovan was gunned downed in Lordsburg."

"Yes sir. A few of the boys overheard the marshal. Is Miss Rachel—?"

"She's unharmed," Hamilton answered. "Meet me in my

study in five minutes." He turned and moved toward the front door. "Yes sir," came the response from behind him. Hamilton heard Elihu spur his horse and gallop away.

"Oh, Hamilton," said Julia, defeated. "I can't lose another."

Hamilton opened the door and looked to her. "We'll bring Rachel back, and apprehend the men who did this."

"My concern is not with those men," she said curtly. She then softened and added, "I just want Rachel returned to us."

"Julia, we won't be able to have one without the other." He then stepped inside and closed the door.

———◆———

Hamilton moved into the study carrying a long leather gun case. He placed it on his desk and pulled out an 1855 Colt revolving 12-gauge shotgun. He held it in his hands and looked it over. Every scuff and nick was a memory. Coming out of his thoughts, he placed it on his desk. He sat and pulled from a drawer a blank piece of stationery. He gazed out the window into the distance for a moment and then retrieved a goose-quill pen from an ink bottle. He began to write.

After a few minutes, he placed the finished note within an envelope as Elihu's penetrating footfalls entered the house. "He's in the study, Elihu," he heard Julia say. "Yes ma'am," came the polite response. Hamilton heard his footsteps draw near. He lifted his eyes to Elihu as the young man appeared and stood in the doorway, hat in hand. He waved him in.

Elihu moved to the center of the room. His eyes fell on the powerful weapon that lay on the desk in front of Hamilton. "I haven't seen you with that Colt shotgun in a while."

His mind focused elsewhere, Hamilton moved past Elihu's comment. "What else did you or the boys hear?"

"Only that Matthew was gunned down by three men," he related. "The deputy's dead, too. Ambushed in a back alley by someone with a Bowie knife, is the thinkin'. Four total."

"I can add," Hamilton said as he lowered his eyes in thought. He opened a desk drawer, pulled out a worn and frayed wanted poster, and pushed it toward Elihu. "I issued this public notice five years ago." He rose and stepped to the window, peering out.

Elihu retrieved the poster. With the words was an illustration of the wanted man. Elihu read the notification aloud.

PROCLAMATION
By HAMILTON PIERCE, the TERRITORIAL
GOVERNOR of ARIZONA
$10,000 REWARD in GOLD COIN
DEAR OR ALIVE!
TY SPOONER
GUNFIGHTER and KNOWN KILLER

"Do you remember this man?" Hamilton asked.

"Ty Spooner," nodded Elihu. "Yes sir, I know of him," he said. "We all do. I heard you speak of him. Caused a lot of trouble while you were territorial governor."

"It ain't much of a likeness, but it's the best I can give you," responded Hamilton. He turned from the window. "I want you to find him."

"Find him?" Elihu repeated in apparent thought. He shook his head. "I heard he was in Mexico, but I wouldn't know—"

"Just south of the border in Sonora," Hamilton interrupted. "Nogales—I heard." He turned from the window to face him. "I want you to ride there, Elihu. If you leave now you'll be there around midnight."

"Yes sir," responded Elihu. "I will take Jess with me. We'll leave quick." He furrowed his brow. "But if I'm riding south, I have one concern—"

"I haven't heard of any trouble at San Carlos," said Hamilton, getting ahead of his question. "The last breakout by the Chiricahua from the reservation was in '81. I don't suspect there will be any more trouble from Geronimo."

"Yes sir," his young ranch foreman responded, with a voice and expression that would lead a listener to believe his concern was now alleviated.

"But—he's proven me wrong before," Hamilton added, having decided to have a little sport with him. "So you let me know if you catch sight of, or are pursued by, him or any other renegade Apache bands when you get back. I will then notify the army, so as to stop the scalpin' and killin' as soon as possible."

"Yes sir," said Elihu again, but this time in a voice and tone that would lead a listener to believe his concern had retaken its place as foremost in his mind. "That'll put a bur under our saddles. We will make good time."

"Good."

Elihu furrowed his brow. "And just exactly what do you want us to do once we find Spooner?"

"I want him to ride with us."

Elihu's eyes fell back on the wanted poster. "You want a man like *this* to ride with us?"

Hamilton took in his concern in thought for he understood it. He turned to gaze back out the window. "Elihu, my life is forfeit when it comes to my daughter. But that's not going to be enough. We're going to need an edge to save her and apprehend or kill these men. Spooner will give us that edge."

"Sir, you made his life a livin' hell while he was on the run. Drove him into Mexico," he reminded him, apparently leading up to what was really on his mind. "I'm a little interested to know why he just won't shoot me when I mention your name?"

Hamilton offered a slight smile as he peered off into the distance. "That's a healthy 'interest' you have there. He turned and observed Elihu with an admiration. "It's just what I would have asked, if I were you," he said, and moved back to his desk. "I've prepared something." He retrieved the sealed envelope from his desk and extended it to him. "Give him this."

Elihu took it in hand.

"It *could* put things in your favor," continued Hamilton. "It contains a letter to Spooner and a few other matters." He retook his seat behind his desk. "Beyond that, you're on your own," he added matter-of-factly. "If you're not back by late afternoon tomorrow, I'll figure the worst and leave without you."

Elihu nodded and stepped toward the doorway. "Lord be with you," came Hamilton's last words to him. Elihu paused at the threshold and glanced back. Hamilton had already removed the five-shot cylinder from the shotgun and began to clean it. "Yes, sir," he responded, then took a deliberate breath and left.

———◆———

A short time later outside the main house, Elihu and Jess were busy with last minute checks of their horses and gear.

"It's a long ride. We'll be riding hard all day," Jess said. "These horses won't be worth a damn once we get there tonight. And neither will our butts."

Satisfied at their preparations, the two men swung up on their mounts. Elihu turned to Jess. "I've got money to pick up fresh horses in Nogales. But that won't help our tail ends. They're just out of luck. Let's go," he said, and they spurred their horses.

Galloping through the Pierce Ranch gate, they left the main house behind them and turned their horses south.

CHAPTER THREE

Graves to Dig

Up a meager rise outside of Lordsburg, the townspeople stood in the cemetery, illuminated by a setting sun. The scattered clouds that hung low on the horizon were blazoned with red, yellow, and orange. The blue and violet hues had already scattered in the distance, no longer falling upon the eyes of the living. Underneath this tinged sky, a graveside memorial service was being held. Those who had gathered formed a solemn circle around the site. Their eyes were upon the open grave, the wooden casket six feet down. Somewhere in the middle of the service, the mourners began to brace themselves against an encroaching chill. A cold November breeze had moved in and swirled about them, no longer kept at bay by the warmth of the overhead sun.

Down the hill Rachel stood dressed in black next to the trunk of a hickory, observing the proceedings. She had placed a hand on the tree with its strong, deep taproots, which gave her support externally and within. She held a rose in her other hand as if she had planned to attend. She heard the town preacher complete the Bible reading, his words drifting down to her. "Now if you'll join me in the hymn 'He Leadeth Me'," she heard him say. It was a hymn familiar to Rachel. Her thoughts drifted away. Before long, she heard them begin the last verse:

> And when my task on earth is done,
> When by thy grace the victory's won,
> E'en death's cold wave I will not flee,
> Since God through Jordan leadeth me.

Rachel placed the rose in a pocket and solemnly moved away, dispensing with the remaining gravesite liturgy. The hymn's words followed her down the small rise.

> He leadeth me, he leadeth me,
> By his own hand he leadeth me;
> His faithful follower I would be,
> For by his hand he leadeth me.

One of the mourners, Ignatius Green, a hefty and well-dressed man of forty-four years, lifted his eyes from the hymnal and observed her moving away. He was a banker and local attorney with the appearance to match. He closed the songbook, stepped away from the circle, and followed Rachel with quick steps down the rise with the obvious intent to catch up with her.

Rachel came off the hill, continuing toward town.

Ignatius hurriedly grew near. "Mrs. Donovan," he said, getting her attention. "Oh, Mrs. Donovan," he beseeched.

She paused and peered back over her shoulder. When he had caught up, she continued on with him walking abreast of her and trying to catch his breath.

"Sorry to disturb your thoughts at a time like this," he said and then gathered another lungful of air, "but I wanted to extend to you my most heartfelt sympathies."

"Thank you, Mr. Green," she responded. "I am glad you stepped forward. I want to engage your bank in settling my husband's estate."

"Yes ma'am," he responded, his breath slowing. "I will handle it personally."

"Basically, I want you to sell everything, Mr. Green. Both real and personal: land, horses, house, furnishings—anything of value," she directed, turning her eyes to him. "Do you understand?"

"Are you sure that is wise?"

She brought her gaze forward once again. "I can no longer bear to be around such things. Ask a fair price and provide me with the receipts . . . less your fee, of course."

"No fee, Mrs. Donovan. You and your late husband have meant a great deal to our community."

27

"Thank you again, Mr. Green. I will use the money to settle my husband's debts."

"Legally, those debts died with your husband," he informed her.

"*I'm* still here, Mr. Green," she responded. "Would an immediate loan from your bank be possible? I would like to purchase provisions," she explained.

"Of course, but may I know why, Mrs. Donovan?"

"Can I confide in you, Mr. Green?"

"Certainly," he assured her. "Our conversation will go no further."

"Good. I'll be staying in town, tonight. I'll be taking a room at the hotel. In the morning, I will be leaving Lordsburg to pursue my husband's killers," she responded matter-of-factly.

Mr. Green stopped in his tracks, obviously taken aback at her response. He peered at her as she moved on. "Oh, my . . ."

Up the rise, silhouetted against the fading light, the minister had finished with the service and the mourners began to disperse and proceed down the hill. Left behind were the figures of two gravediggers. One sat on the ground, and the other leaned against a tree, his shovel at his side. The two had dug the hole and now they must refill it. The one standing straightened from the tree and stepped over to the grave. The darkened shape then jabbed his shovel into the nearby piled earth and put a boot to the back of the tool, pushing it deeper, and began tossing in spadefuls into the open grave. The other silhouetted man got to his feet, and they both went back to work.

———•———

Elihu and Jess rode their horses through the darkness of the desert. The same setting sun that had given fading light to the mourners in Lordsburg had taken its bow many hours ago. The grand painted sky that had illuminated the desert and western mountains on the last leg of their journey had long ago exited, giving way to moonlight, darkness, and shadows.

Elihu brought his horse down to a walk and Jess did the same.

"Let's rest 'em," Elihu said.

After a moment, Jess spoke up. "So you think Mr. Pierce was greenin' ya about Geronimo," he commented, as if they'd already had words on the subject.

Elihu nodded. "I was a little slow in my thinkin', but yep." He then smiled as if in memory. "Just like he used to when I first started working for him. I was real raw back then. And it was his way of teaching me things I needed to know."

"Do you think Mr. Pierce would have sent us if he *really* thought there was a possibility we could encounter renegade Chiricahua?" Jess asked.

"Yep—in a heartbeat," Elihu responded. "It's all about weighing one matter against another. I would have volunteered to go, anyway. I think a lot of Miss Rachel."

"It's good to know we won't discover Geronimo or his band peekin' out from behind the saguaro."

"Yep—but I do have my long underwear on, though."

Jess glanced to him. "Now why would you do that?"

"It is true, Geronimo's at San Carlos, but there are the *other* renegade Chiricahua bands Mr. Pierce spoke of. Could be one of them has gone to scalpin' those they find and stakin' them out in the sun—naked. I plan to appeal to their mercies. They've been known to let you keep your long underwear on. Did I forget to tell ya to bring yours?"

Jess smiled as if he knew he was being sported with. "Yeah, well, I thought ahead too—I brought a razor. First sight of them I'll be bald as a cue ball before you know it. And, no, you can't borrow it. A razor is a personal thing. Besides, that way they'll concentrate on you more than me. It could give me a chance to get away, which will make you feel better not havin' told me to bring long underwear."

Elihu smiled. "Bald or not, they're going to be more interested in you."

"And why's that?" Jess asked casually.

Elihu motioned to the back of Jess's saddle. "Due to that Chiricahua scalp."

With a furrowed brow, Jess peered back to see to what he was referring.

Elihu shook his head. "With it danglin' like that for all to see—it will really get their attention."

Jess's eyes grew wide. "What the hell!" he said, as he swatted the hairpiece off.

"I put it on there when we stopped to eat and rest the horses."

"That ain't funny!" Jess shot back, his words angry and a little frightened. "Could be there *are* some Apaches around here," he proclaimed, his tone dismayed. "If they had found that, they'd have tortured me for days!"

"Or—it could be that was just horsehair I cut from your horse's tail."

Jess calmed and shook his head. "*Greenin'* people must run in the family—so to speak."

"Tell me," Elihu continued, amused, "while they were torturin' you for days, did I get away in that little scenario of yours—like I had planned?"

"Yeah, you got away. But my dead ghost caught up with ya—and it was a sight!"

Elihu laughed good-naturedly and dug spur. Jess followed.

———◆———

Rachel pushed aside the curtains in her second-story hotel window and peered down into the darkened street and the night beyond. She was still wearing her black mourning dress. She let the curtains drop and stepped over to the dresser, where she had placed a lantern and her purchases from this morning that had been collected off the boardwalk and returned to her. She positioned one of the candles she had bought inside the lantern and placed the other in her pocket.

Rachel emerged from the hotel with the lantern in hand. Striking a match on a post, she lit the candle within and stepped into the darkened street.

Soon she was making her way up the hill to the cemetery, her black dress blending with the night. In one hand was the lantern—in the other, the rose she held earlier.

Back in town, Ignatius Green caught sight of the lantern from his second-story residence above his office. He peered out the window solemnly, watching the lantern move up the hill as if he knew who was carrying it.

Rachel entered the cemetery, holding the lantern high for direction and so as not to make a misstep on uneven ground or stumble over grave markers. She approached her husband's newly filled grave and peered down at the temporary wooden marker, the glow from the lantern illuminating her mourning dress. She placed the lamp down and then knelt.

"I wanted to say some words to you—some private words I couldn't say earlier with everyone gathered," she said, speaking as if Matthew were there. "I'm going to pursue those men. And I wanted to tell you why, for I know you would not approve." She lowered her eyes for a moment, then raised them. "Vengeance," she said simply. "I will seek retribution, Matthew. Such matters I would usually leave to others. But there are no others riding in pursuit of these men. Knowing my father, he will be coming quick from Arizona to join me, but it will be another full day or more before he gets here. I cannot let the trail of those murderers disappear." After a moment, she continued apologetically. "Again, I know that is not what you would want." She then offered a slight smile. "But you married me for better or worse."

Rachel then removed the other candle from her pocket and placed it before her husband's marker. "As I promised you this morning," she said as she lit the candle. After a long moment, she retrieved the lantern, and rose to her feet. She peered down at the grave a last time, then turned and moved back through the cemetery.

———◆———

In the same late-night darkness, Elihu and Jess approached the outskirts of a small Mexican village. They pulled up.

"Nogales?" Jess asked.

"I sure hope so," Elihu responded.

They spurred lightly and continued on.

"What time do you reckon it is?" asked Jess.

"Midnight would be a fair guess."

In their sight, between them and the village, was a cemetery. In this graveyard they could see a boy holding a lantern for a man digging a grave. The boy stood patiently by while the laboring man tossed spadefuls of dirt. Next to them was a donkey and cart.

Elihu and Jess approached slowly as much from weariness as caution. With eyes on the cart, they paused before the boy and man. The boy's lantern light spilled over two dead men in the wagon, their hands folded across their chests. Both had obviously died violently from shotgun wounds.

The boy peered up at them. The man continued to dig. Neither seemed concerned as to who the strangers were or cared that they were there.

Elihu took notice of the makeshift headstone made of old planks that lay nearby. "There are no words on the marker," he said to the boy.

The boy frowned. "It is my job to add the epitaph," he explained. "But I don't know what to say. Maybe you can help me," he added hopefully.

"Who were they?" asked Elihu.

The boy shrugged. "They were bad men. They deserved to die. They were cast out of Paradise."

"Paradise?" repeated Jess, taken aback.

The boy nodded and moved on to another subject. "We really don't bury them six feet down." He glanced to the struggling gravedigger. "We are paid to, but my father gets tired."

"He's your father?" came back Jess in a surprised tone.

The boy nodded.

"He keeps you workin' late," said Jess in an amiable manner.

"It is hot in Nogales," the boy explained. "We must take care of them before they smell."

The man digging the grave continued to dig and toss dirt.

"Who put them in this condition?" Elihu asked.

"Must have been a vaquero meaner than they were," Jess commented.

"*El Diablo Tejano*," responded the boy, nodding. "He is my friend," he added with pride.

"The Texas Devil?" said Elihu, translating. He straightened in the saddle, stretching his weary bones. "Well . . ." he said, getting back to the business at hand, "we're looking for a man—goes by the name Spooner."

The man digging the grave tossed a spadeful of dirt and paused. He pulled a bandana and wiped his brow. "*Si, el Diablo Tejano.*"

Elihu and Jess glanced to one another, then returned their gaze to the gravedigger. "Spooner did this?" Elihu asked, taken aback.

The gravedigger nodded. "*Si, si.*" He motioned into the village. "*En la cantina.*"

Elihu and Jess looked to the lantern-lit village.

"Which one would that be?" Jess asked.

"Paradise," the boy responded.

"Like you said," Elihu responded with a wry smile. "They were cast out of Paradise."

"Are you looking for trouble?" asked the boy. "Should I have a cart ready for you, *Señors*?"

35

At this morbid thought, Elihu and Jess glanced at one another again. Elihu flipped the boy a silver dollar coin and they spurred on toward the village.

"A whole dollar!" The grateful boy jumped on a nearby headstone with the lantern held high and called after them, "For this I will make sure there is a blanket in the cart for your comfort. And bury you before you smell."

CHAPTER FOUR

Entering Paradise

Elihu and Jess walked their horses into the old Spanish village. The only commerce at this hour were the cantinas that dotted the darkened street. Up head, the light from within these establishments spilled out. The eyes of the two men took in everything as they moved deeper into town. The illumination from lanterns and torches danced across the adobe frames, creating shadows within which darkened figures could be seen. A few of the Mexicans who called Nogales home, and those who were just passing through, stepped along the boardwalk, moving from one cantina to another. They eyed the *Norte Americanos* with apparent suspicion.

Elihu and Jess passed the cantinas one by one, their eyes searching. Spanish piano music and song emanated, mixing with drunken laughter and conversation in both Spanish and English. Elihu's eyes fell upon a sight up ahead, and pulled up, as did Jess. "There's Paradise," he said, reading the sign above the cantina.

Jess looked to the establishment with the word painted in English above the entrance and sighed. "It's definitely not the great reward my mama described to me as a boy."

They urged their horses forward, angling them toward "Paradise."

As they approached, Jess grimaced and shook his head as if the music he was hearing was offensive to his ear drums. "Is it my ears, or is it the—?"

"It's the piano," Elihu interjected, letting him know he agreed with him. "It's out of tune."

"Or the one banging on its keys."

They dismounted and tied off. Elihu opened his saddle bag and pulled out the envelope Hamilton had given him. He folded it and tucked it in his waistband. The two men stepped up onto the boardwalk and paused to look to one another, apparently burnishing their courage. Elihu took a deliberate breath and moved forward to enter the cantina.

Elihu pushed through the door and Jess followed. They took a few steps in and stopped to look around the dimly lit establishment. All about were male and female patrons influenced by tequila and whiskey. A smiling piano player at an aged piano banged on the ivory keys, happily oblivious to the succession of sour notes, or just did not care. Elihu and Jess stepped toward the bar. They casually peered about, but with an undertone of caution, as they looked for someone who might fit the description of whom they had been sent to find.

The patrons returned their looks with evident curiosity and distrust.

Reaching the bar, Elihu exhaled and leaned an elbow on it.

Jess placed both hands on the smoothed wood surface as if steadying himself.

Elihu casually looked to the man tending bar at the other end. "Tequila," he called out, ordering for him and Jess. He turned to his friend, "What do you think?" he asked in a low voice "Did you see him?"

Jess gave a quick shake of his head and looked again over his shoulder. "Don't know." He then motioned to a back corner. "That could be him."

The bartender approached and pulled a bottle and shot glasses from underneath the bar. He placed them in front of his new customers and poured. Elihu pushed money, and then he and Jess placed hands and eyes on their drinks, as if the tequila needed to be admired first.

Jess looked to the bartender and smiled. "This tequila would taste sweeter if that piano was in tune."

They lifted their glasses and pulled them close.

With their gun hands busy, the bartender smoothly pulled a double-barrel shotgun from behind the bar, cocked both barrels, and leveled it at Elihu and Jess. Their mouths open, the two men froze with drinks in hand just short of their destinations, their eyes on the open end of the large-bore weapon pointed at them.

An old man at the end of the bar chuckled in his drink. "*El Diablo Tejano*"

Jess lifted his eyes from the two barrels to the man who was holding the weapon. "I sure didn't mean anything by it, mister," Jess offered, swallowing hard. "On second thought, that piano sounds as sweet as an angel's voice in paradise."

"Who are you men and what is your business here?" asked the bartender who had just poured their drinks. He was a tall man of forty-three years. He had good features blended with a hardness of time and experience. With his eyes locked on them, he presented a firmness of manner that came with a guarantee of action.

The once lively cantina conversation dwindled away to silence.

Elihu pulled in air, restarting his breathing. "Mister, my name is Elihu Merritt. This here is Jess Whitt," he added with a head nod. "We were sent here to find somebody, that's all. We are definitely not looking for trouble."

Jess quickly spoke up. "That's right—just lookin' for someone. Nothin' more."

"Put your guns on the bar and step back," the bartender said.

"Mister, whatever you want," responded Elihu. He and Jess placed their drinks and guns on the bar and took a step back.

"Who you looking for?" asked the man with the shotgun.

"A man by the name of Ty Spooner," responded Elihu. "We were told by a boy and his father digging a grave outside of town that he might be here in this cantina."

"I'm Spooner."

"Yes sir," said Elihu. "I'm figurin' as much, now. That makes twice today I was a little late in my thinkin'. We were sent here to talk with you."

"Who sent ya?"

"Mr. Hamilton Pierce of the Pierce Ranch up Tucson way," Elihu responded. "He wants you to ride with him in pursuit of killers."

"How did he know I wouldn't just shoot you where ya stand?"

"Mister, I got no guarantees there. But I was to give you this envelope," he said, motioning to it in his waistband. "If I may."

Ty nodded.

Elihu pulled the envelope and extended it. "Rachel's husband—his daughter's husband—was murdered in Lordsburg. He was the marshal there."

"Open it and empty it on the bar."

Elihu stepped forward and proceeded to do what he was told. Among the spilled contents were an old newspaper clipping, a daguerreotype, and Hamilton's handwritten note. Before stepping back, Elihu glanced down at the faded newspaper clipping from Gonzales, Texas.

VICTORY AT THE BATTLE OF
RIO GRANDE CITY!!
The End of the Cortina War

Dec. 27, 1859. Hometown boys Hamilton Pierce and Ty Spooner—now Texas Rangers recruited by Captain John 'Rip' Ford—took part in the crushing defeat of the Cortinistas. Along with the US 2nd Cavalry, the Texas Rangers forced partisan leader Juan Cortina to flee back to Mexico on horseback. Many of his men jumped into the Rio Grande . . . .

Elihu stared in disbelief. "You were a Texas Ranger. Well, I'll be—"

Ty motioned with his shotgun for Elihu to go quiet and step back, which he did promptly, rejoining Jess. He put the shotgun on the bar with the barrels facing them and gathered the contents from the envelope. He glanced at the newspaper clipping Elihu was reading, then tossed it back on the bar. He peered thoughtfully at the daguerreotype for a long moment and put it in his shirt pocket. As he began to read Hamilton's note, he looked up to the men who stood unmoving, their eyes on him. He motioned to their glasses on the bar. "Your tequila," he said, indicating they could take their drinks in hand once again. "You paid for it." He then added, "Your guns stay where they are."

Elihu and Jess glanced to one another, then stepped forward and quickly threw back the very much welcomed spirits.

"Got money for fresh horses?" Ty asked.

Elihu nodded.

"Get two hours rest—then we leave."

———————◆———————

Elihu and Jess emerged from the Paradise cantina. Ty followed. The piano player was once again filling the night air with sour notes from the old piano. Three fresh horses had been saddled and were waiting. Elihu and Jess mounted, and Ty swung up into his saddle. Elihu and Jess had their guns back in holster.

The sound of a squeaky wheel approached unseen in the darkness from down the street.

Elihu turned his gaze to it, trying to make it out. "You lead," he heard Ty say. Elihu swung his gaze back to Ty, who motioned them forward. He and Jess turned their reins and pointed their horses back the way they had come and, now, toward the squeaky wheel that was coming ever closer.

"What is that?" Jess asked. "It's as bad as that piano."

Out of the darkness and into the torch light, the grave-digger and the boy emerged. The father was wearily pushing the cart they had seen—its squeak preceding them, heralding their approach.

"It's that buryin' cart," Elihu said.

At the sight of Elihu and Jess on their horses—alive and otherwise unharmed—the gravedigger sighed with evident disappointment, turned his blood-stained cart back around, and moved slowly away.

Elihu and Jess pulled up and looked to the boy.

"We wanted to come by the cantina—just in case," the boy explained.

"Just in case?" Elihu inquired, as the gravedigger with his squeaky wheel disappeared back into the shadows of the street once again.

"Just in case you were cast out of Paradise, too," the boy said, and then shrugged. "It was my idea. Business is business," he added, smiling. "No offense, *señor*."

"None taken," Elihu said, returning his smile. "It shows initiative." He flipped another silver dollar to the boy. "You came *real* close to being right."

Soon Elihu and Jess were on the outskirts, stepping their horses past the graveyard in the darkness. Ty followed behind. The cemetery was now quiet. The boy and his father had completed their job—their money earned. In their place was a freshly filled-in grave for two with the wood-planked marker firmly planted overtop. A freshly painted epitaph could be seen in the moonlight. As Elihu and Jess passed by, their eyes dropped to the marker. It read: "*Tres Pies Hacia Abajo y El Infierno Para Ir.*"

"Well, the boy finally chose some words for the two men they buried," Jess commented. "What does it say?" he asked Elihu.

"Three feet down and Hell to go."

CHAPTER FIVE

If You End Up Dead—No Deal

Ignatius Green emerged from a merchant store and began to cross the street. He squinted in the early morning light and paused as he noticed something. He held a hand to his eyes to shield the sun. In his sight, Rachel was outside a supply store loading provisions onto her horse.

Rachel closed her saddle bag and secured the flap. She was outfitted in trail clothes and a cross-draw holster for her gun. She pulled from the holster a .36 caliber Colt 1862 Pocket Navy revolver her father had given her years ago. Checking its load, she paused to admire the gun in thought and remembrance. She looked at the engraved stagecoach holdup scene on its cylinder, which was at odds with its name, "Navy." She recalled her father telling her that the original Colt 1851 model depicted a naval battle from which it garnered its name. The name stuck and stayed with the release of the newer model. Coming out of her thoughts, she reholstered it, and mounted her horse. Her husband's Winchester protruded from the saddle scabbard. She turned her horse and then saw Mr. Green's approach.

"Good morning, Mrs. Donovan," he said with a smile, which faded when he caught sight of her clothes and the arms she was carrying. "Yes, well—I just stepped over to tell you that your property will sell quickly," he said, in the manner of someone delivering good news. "There have already been inquiries," he added, his words suddenly trailing off as he realized the callousness. "My apologies. Commerce can be insensitive," he offered as explanation.

"It's what I wanted. Have everything ready upon my return," Rachel said, as she lifted the reins, preparing to move on.

"Yes, ma'am," he responded agreeably, but in a way that made her turn her gaze back to him.

Rachel could tell by his eyes and demeanor that he wanted to say more, but the courage wasn't there. She knew him to be a gentleman and knew there was a question he wanted to ask, but he was being sensitive to her. "Your next question should have been, Mr. Green," she said to him, helping him through it, "'and if you don't return?'"

Apparently uneasy, the man's gaze dropped to the ground.

"If it has been so determined to your satisfaction that I am dead," she instructed, "send all proceeds to my father Hamilton Pierce in Tucson. If he's dead, then to Julia, his wife and my mother."

The banker lifted his eyes to her and nodded in solemn response.

She urged her horse forward. "Good day, Mr. Green."

Rachel walked her horse out of town. The townspeople took notice. When she passed by the telegraph office, the clerk to whom she had dictated her urgent message yesterday morning hurried outside to watch. Rachel passed the ground where her husband had lain dying. Then she passed Hannah Bristow, who had risked her life that morning by stepping into the street and denouncing Matthew's killer.

Hannah stepped off the boardwalk to address Rachel as she rode past. "You take care of yourself, Rachel Donovan," she called out with apparent pride in the woman she was observing.

As she neared the outskirts of Lordsburg, Rachel had the horse pick up its gait. Outside of town, she turned east and spurred her horse.

———————

Just past mid-afternoon, Elihu and Jess rode forward of Ty through the expanse and grandeur of the Arizona terrain. The sagebrush and saguaro transitioned to the magnificent green foothills of the Santa Catalina Mountains.

Up ahead, a ranch hand approached at a gallop. Elihu spurred his horse to meet him. After a brief discussion, the ranch hand rode off in a hurry and Elihu returned. "We're running the south herd over to Bull's Head Slough," he informed Jess. "Should be water enough there—maybe." He noticed Ty looking around, his eyes taking in the vast land abounding with cattle and horses.

"J-connected-H," Ty said, reading the brand on the animals' hides. "Julia and Hamilton."

"Yep," Elihu responded. His eyes then swept the land. "They're all his—as far as you can see," he stated with pride. "The Pierce Ranch is just over that hill," he informed him, motioning. He then took a deliberate breath and swung his eyes to Ty. "Are you going to follow Jess and me all the way there?"

Ty offered a smile. He brought his horse up to theirs, and they all spurred forward.

Before long, they trotted under the wrought-iron entrance gate proclaiming the Pierce Ranch, and then up the tree-lined route to the main house. Ranch hands broke off from what they were doing and ran and jumped up on a nearby fence, hollering in welcome.

Hamilton was at his desk in his study and heard the commotion. He rose, stepped over to the window, and peered out. He saw one of his ranch hands gallop up to the house waving his hat.

"Elihu and Jess are back," the cowboy shouted, heralding their arrival. "And they got him with 'em."

Hamilton emerged onto the porch, stepping forward into the sun and taking a commanding stance at the edge of the steps. He observed as the men rode up three abreast—

his gaze on Ty. With a firmness of manner, Hamilton's eyes searched the visage of this man whom he hadn't been face-to-face with in years. From their youthful friendship to later conflict of the worst kind, he stood remembering this man from out of the past.

Elihu and Jess swung down from their saddles.

Ty made no such move—his eyes on Hamilton. His spirited mount reflected the conflict and dynamics of these two men coming together once again. Its head bobbed with nostrils flared, drawing in air, filling its lungs. Wide-eyed, the magnificent animal stomped and pawed, its body gleaming with sweat from a hurried ride.

Hamilton swung his eyes to Elihu and Jess. "Good work, boys. You made good time."

Elihu glanced back at Ty. "We damned near ended up in a graveyard outside of Nogales, bewilderin' a Mexican boy and his gravedigger father as to what to write on our marker."

From this, Hamilton knew Elihu and Jess had a story to tell for later. "I'm sure he would have come up with somethin' to your liking," he said, amused at the way Elihu expressed himself. He turned a hard gaze back to Ty for a few moments and said, "Less than two days ago, my son-in-law lost his life. I can't do anything about that. If it were me, I would just let God, or the law, take the men responsible, whichever came first." He stepped off the porch and continued. "Rachel, though, has decided to hurry that justice along. She has gone in pursuit of these killers. Now

I need your help to find her and the men she is after." At this, Hamilton's story telling was over. He took on a strictly businesslike tone and manner and added, "In the note I sent, I made you an offer. By being here, I assume you find it acceptable."

"Good to see small talk hasn't dirtied up your conversation any," Ty said.

Nearby, several ranch hands were gathering around a fence to observe the proceedings. Some leaned against the posts while others took seat on the top rail to give scrutiny to Ty—the outlaw they had heard so much about. Tired and dusty, they had taken a brief break from their responsibilities. Seated on a top fence rail was Seth Garrett, a man of twenty-one years, whose manner seemed stamped with bitterness and frustration. "I always thought a lot of Rachel," he said in a low voice to the cowboy next to him.

Jess approached and leaned on the fence near Seth. He hooked a boot heel on a fence rail; his gaze on Ty and Hamilton.

A nearby cowboy turned to Jess. "You have any trouble with Spooner in Nogales?"

"He pulled a shotgun on us."

Seth turned his gaze to Jess.

Jess continued, "We were in a bar about to take a drink of tequila when we were suddenly looking down both barrels. That buckshot would have been a helluva chaser."

At this, Seth turned a disdainful gaze to Ty.

Hamilton stepped closer to the man on a horse before him. "You know this man De La Rosa?"

"No—heard of him, though," Ty responded. "A pistolero. Mean."

"As long as I keep my Rachel from harm, I don't care how we do this." He then paused and took a breath. "I will restate the deal offered. As specified in my letter, when the job is done, I will arrange a pardon from the territorial governor and provide you a sum of one thousand dollars. I figure you are compensated fairly." At this, Hamilton turned and began to move back up the steps to the porch.

"I figure different."

Hamilton whirled back around and met Ty's eyes once again.

On the fence, Seth glared at Ty, his obvious frustration growing. "A thousand dollars! Damn!" he exclaimed, under his breath. "Mr. Pierce should offer *me* the money. I can handle a gun as good as most. At least as good as some *former* gunfighter."

"Mr. Pierce knows what he's doing," came the response of the cowboy next to him.

"Are you saying I'm not good enough?"

"Just saying he knows what's best—that's all."

At this, Seth jumped down off the fence and proceeded toward Ty.

Hamilton moved back down the steps and took a firm stance before Ty. "We're talking about my daughter's life!"

"I'm a little more concerned about my own, right now."

"How much do you want?" Hamilton asked incredulously. "I'm taking the rope from around your neck and giving you money to start a new life. Ten years ago you would risk your life for a few hundred dollars in a train robbery. You trying to say you hold life more dear now?"

Seth moved in, his eyes on Ty, his posture challenging. "What makes this *barkeep* so good, Mr. Pierce? Any man can pull a shotgun, as he did on Elihu and Jess."

Elihu quickly stepped forward. "Seth!"

Seth continued, "You'll need a man that can handle a short gun, Mr. Pierce—I can. Maybe I should show you and Mr. Spooner here," he added with disdain.

Ty calmly observed the young man.

"Damn it!" Elihu quickly mounted his horse and spurred him between Seth and Ty.

"Collect your things and get off my land, Mr. Garrett," Hamilton said firmly.

The response obviously unexpected to Seth, he turned to Hamilton.

"Elihu, square with him his due wages," Hamilton instructed.

"Yes sir," Elihu replied, as he peered down at Seth from his saddle.

"But, Mr. Pierce—" pleaded Seth.

"John Milby's ranch could use a good hand," Hamilton said. "I suggest you start there."

Seth took this in. He then took a breath and moved away with anger written on his face. Elihu followed him on his horse.

Not taking his eyes off Seth, Ty watched him leave.

"Elihu can handle him," said Hamilton, noticing Ty's caution.

Ty swung his gaze back to Hamilton. "The kind of men you're after ain't going to throw their hands up when you catch 'em, or give a damn that you're *the* Hamilton Pierce. And they've got friends everywhere. I don't give us much chance."

Hamilton nodded. "All right—I'm asking you again, you son of a bitch. What do you want?"

Ty straightened in his saddle and peered about. "You look prosperous enough. I heard so."

"That's none of your concern."

"There's a direction I'm going with it."

"Get to it!"

"When you first broke ground, I helped you hold your stake in this land."

"I remember."

My price is twenty-five percent ownership of the Pierce Ranch."

"You son of a bitch!" came the quick reply. "Twenty-five percent of everything I've worked hard for! I ought to string you up right here and now!"

Ty jerked his reins to leave.

"Turn that horse back around!"

Ty reined in his defiant mount.

Hamilton calmed his manner. It was a protest he knew he couldn't back up. He peered at Ty, attempting to read the man he once knew so well. He took in his words and manner and came to a conclusion about him. "You need to allow me enough rope to buck and kick some," Hamilton said finally. In an appeal, he stepped closer for emphasis, his demeanor now conciliatory. "Without Rachel, this ranch—this land," he began as his eyes swept the Catalina foothills before them, "means nothing to me or Julia." He returned his gaze to Ty. "You've got your deal, but only if Rachel returns alive."

Ty nodded.

Hamilton took a breath and added. "But you listen closely," he started as he took a step closer, "if you end up dead, even by the last bullet—no deal. We won't be beholden to any kin of yours. Do you understand?"

"Fair enough." With the deal done, Ty turned back to business. "I asked around in Nogales. Tom Braden, out of Texas, helps lead the bunch with De La Rosa. Most likely heading that way. They're real good at what they do—stealing horses and running them south across the border. Your son-in-law was becoming an interference."

Hamilton nodded. "I've got fifteen men that will ride with us."

"We'll take your best two—no more."

"Two?" he shot back, questioning his logic.

"You take fifteen men, they'll put an ear to the ground

and hightail it to Mexico," Ty explained. "With four, they won't be so skittish. They'd sooner just kill us than run."

"Makes sense—should have thought of it myself." Hamilton turned to Elihu. "Pick out one man and include yourself."

"Yes sir!" He then quickly called out, "Jess!"

Jess unhooked his boot and pushed away from the fence, his eyes on Elihu.

"You're ridin'," Elihu informed him.

Jess nodded eagerly and quickly moved away.

Hamilton turned to the ranch hands nearby. "The rest of ya stay here." He then directed his words to Ty and Elihu. "We're leaving for Tucson immediately. We'll be there in time to take the last train out. We'll provision in Tucson. It'll be the middle of the night when we get to Lordsburg and I don't want to wake up any store keepers." With eyes on Elihu, he added, "I know you're tired. You and Jess can get some rest on the train." He turned to Ty. "What kind of chance do you think Rachel has?"

"You tell me."

———◆———

Outside the main house, Ty, Elihu, and Jess were mounted on fresh horses and ready to leave. Elihu held the reins of Hamilton's horse. Julia was on the porch, awaiting Hamilton. He emerged, striding forward with purpose. She intercepted. "Hamilton—"

"We'll get her back, Julia," he assured her, attempting to

deflect any concern she might express for him. "That I promise."

"You're a worthy man, Hamilton, and I'm a blessed woman for having been with you all these years."

He tried to brush off her worry and move past.

She gripped his arm.

He turned fully to her.

"But I'm not ready to be alone," she said. "That time will come too soon as it is. I'll be waiting for the return of both of you."

Hamilton kissed her and started away. She held firm on his arm one more time and said, "Rachel grew up wild on this ranch after her brother died. She took his place and worked hard side by side with you. She's got a lot of you in her and some of me. She'll be needing that part of you now, more than ever."

Hamilton took in her words and nodded. His eyes stayed on her, her grip still firm.

She finally loosened her hold.

He gave her a quick reassuring smile and moved off the porch.

"Elihu," he called out, asking as to their preparedness.

"Ready, Mr. Pierce."

Hamilton mounted his horse and turned to face Ty. Answering his earlier question, he said, "Rachel can handle herself. I made sure of that." He looked to Julia one last time and spurred his horse. The others followed.

Julia watched as they galloped down the tree-lined entranceway and passed under the arched gate. Shen bowed her head momentarily, then turned to move inside.

CHAPTER SIX

A Woman of Hardy Stock

With the sun low, Hamilton and Ty rode ahead of Elihu and Jess as they walked their horses through the streets of Tucson. Hamilton pulled up across from the sheriff's office and looked back to Elihu. "Check with the sheriff to see if there's anything else we should know. Maybe he has some new information on De La Rosa."

Elihu nodded, turned his horse, and stepped over to the office. He dismounted and proceeded onto the boardwalk.

"Elihu," Hamilton said, getting his attention.

He turned.

"And let the sheriff know I have *the* Ty Spooner with me. And let him know why." He then rested his eyes on Ty and continued his instructions to Elihu. "We don't want to suffer any delays due to a lawman or some upstanding citizen attempting to do the right thing and *hang him* for his past deeds, now do we?" he asked wryly.

59

Ty met Hamilton's eyes.

"Yes sir!—I mean, no sir," Elihu responded, and entered the sheriff's office.

Hamilton turned to Jess. "Get our supplies. I'll be at the bank withdrawing traveling money."

"Yes sir!" Jess responded with an eagerness and spurred off.

"You took to barkin' orders really well, since the last time I saw ya'," Ty said. He then straightened in the saddle and added, "I'll be at the depot acquiring tickets—that is, if you don't have an objection."

"Would it do any good?" Hamilton shot back sarcastically, and then turned his gaze from him in thought momentarily. When he turned back and saw Ty still there, he said quickly, "Well, what are ya waitin' on!"

Ty offered a wry smile, gave a light spur and moved away.

Hamilton then swung his eyes to the bank down the street and urged his horse forward.

Ty moved through the busy town. He observed the townspeople and they—him. He projected the natural, easy confidence of a man who could handle himself. As he passed, the townspeople's eyes expressed the observance of someone who appeared to belong to a more dangerous world and was intruding on theirs. With it, they seemed to project respect and fear, along with a certain apparent bewilderment of not really knowing why.

Ty approached the train depot and dismounted. He stepped up onto the platform and approached a window that proclaimed TICKETS overhead. A passenger in front of him completed a purchase, then Ty stepped up to the clerk.

"Yes, yes, let's move along," the ticket clerk said, his words clipped and hurried. "How may I help you?" he asked, his manner and tone projecting a high degree of polished efficiency.

"Four men and horses to Lordsburg."

The clerk nodded and began to see to his request.

Stepping up behind Ty on the platform was Tennessee Jane Dancer, a pretty woman of twenty-three years, who was of obvious wealth and breeding. She approached and took her place in line behind Ty.

The ticket clerk looked up from his tabulating and nodded past Ty. "Good seeing you again, Mrs. Dancer." He returned to the task at hand. "Let's see . . . four conveyances to Lordsburg, New Mexico Territory, plus horses, which will, of course, be an additional charge—"

"How much?"

The ticket clerk paused, took a breath, and directed Ty to the sign that listed fares and extra charges. "It would have been more efficient if you had taken note beforehand," he said, then went back to his tabulating. "That will be twenty dollars," he informed him, finishing up.

Ty pushed money.

The clerk produced the tickets and pushed them to Ty,

casting a judgmental eye on him. "The Southern Pacific does offer a discount on roundtrip tickets." He then added with apparent disdain, "Very advantageous for those who, shall we say . . . are lacking funds."

"How much?"

"Well then, I will *have* to re-tabulate, won't I?" he said, taking pencil in hand once again. "That will be four returning?" he inquired.

"Don't know."

The railroad employee paused, his eyes on his note pad. With pursed lips, he began tapping his pencil on the tablet, and then lifted irritated eyes to Ty.

"It would depend on how many of us get there alive, wouldn't it? Trains are dangerous: derailments, Indians, runaway engines. We are hopeful that most of us will make it—God willin'," he said, having sport with him, though undetectable to the efficient clerk.

Startled at his response, the ticket clerk stammered.

Ty retrieved the one-way tickets. "Yes, perhaps it's better the return tickets be purchased in Lordsburg. We'll know then if our count stays whole at four and that we hadn't lost anyone on the way. If so, we would then, of course, need to make arrangements for casket transport back to Tucson. And before I do, I will, of course, make note of the sign that lists fares and extra charges for those that are dead and gone, who, having a misplaced trust, had their lives concluded while traveling on the Southern Pacific."

The wide-eyed clerk stared back at him. Along the way, as Ty's words progressed, all his pretentious behavior left and was replaced with a scandalized deportment.

Having wiped the arrogance and irritation from the clerk's visage, Ty tipped his hat. "Much obliged," he said, and stepped away.

Alarmed, Tennessee's eyes followed Ty as he moved past her. She stepped forward to the window and addressed the ticket clerk. "What did he mean?" she asked, with evident concern.

The ticket clerk was beside himself. "P-please, Mrs. Dancer, I can assure you there is no reason for alarm. Our trains are perfectly safe."

She turned her eyes back in the direction of Ty, who was moving away on his horse. "Some people!" she exclaimed with apparent disgust.

"Such men are a hazard of my job," the ticket clerk informed her. "I do hope you will not let this incident affect your travel or otherwise affect your opinion of the Southern Pacific. We do appreciate your and your husband's business."

"I have learned not to let such men affect me," she responded, with her eyes still on Ty. "After all, we women of hardy stock are capable and competent when facing adversity."

Rachel leaned forward in her saddle and peered into the distance of New Mexico Territory, her eyes intently focused. She observed four cowboys breaking horses at a campsite, but they were not the men she saw that morning in Lordsburg. "Come on, Jolie," she said, urging her horse forward.

The bronc busters had now stopped to take a meal. They were carrying their tin plates and eating utensils and finding a place to sit on the ground. They noticed a rider slowly approaching their camp and kept their eyes in that direction as they spooned their beans, taking in mouthfuls as big as they could manage.

Rachel ambled her horse up. "Hello in the camp," she said in greeting.

"Would you look at that," said one cowboy, apparently floored at the uncommon sight of an attractive woman trail rider. One paused his spoonful in mid gulp while another, with his mouth already full, just stopped chewing and stared. One bronc buster put down his plate, stood, and wiped his mouth. "Well, hello!" he grinned, his smile pushing up into his eyes.

She spoke up. "I'm looking for four men who—"

"You don't have to look any further," the standing bronc buster said. "You've found 'em!"

"You don't understand," she responded.

Still grinning, the bronc buster approached her.

The leader of the bronc busters observed. He shook his head, put his plate aside, and got to his feet. "Josh!" he said, in a scolding manner.

The bronc buster put his hand on Rachel's leg. "Why don't you just get off that horse and right onto my lap—"

Rachel quickly pulled her Colt revolver from her cross-draw holster and struck him hard across the face with its barrel, knocking him back a few feet, where he stumbled to the ground, landing on his butt, when his boot heel caught a stone. She cocked the revolver and aimed it in the direction of the others. "Son of a bitch!" she said in disbelief.

The leader raised his hands to calm the situation. "Hold on! Hold on!"

She turned her gaze to the leader. "You will make a big mistake if you think I can't use this."

"He was just trying to be friendly."

"This isn't a saloon!" she shot back angrily. "And I am no prostitute he can paw!"

"I admit he's not too bright, but he ain't worth shootin', neither," the leader responded.

"Now I will ask you again—I'm looking for four men who might have come this way. One goes by the name Juan de La Rosa. Have you come across them?"

Excited, another bronc buster tossed aside his plate and quickly mounted up. "Whew! Ain't she somethin'!" he exclaimed.

"Yeah!" yelled the fourth one, excitement filling his voice. "I think we need to herd her in!"

The mounted bronc buster spurred his horse toward

Rachel. He reared up his mount, intending to spook her horse and throw her.

The leader stepped forward. "No! Damn it!"

Rachel's horse reared. Afraid that she'd be thrown and be at the mercy of these men, she fired, shooting the offending cowboy's horse. The dying horse and its rider tumbled backwards.

The leader threw his hat to the ground in frustration. "Damn!"

Rachel pulled the hammer back on her Navy Colt.

Obviously surprised and humiliated, the felled bronc buster started to rise and draw his weapon.

"You damn fool!" yelled the leader.

The hammer dropped on Rachel's Colt, and the .36 caliber gunfire ripped into the shoulder of the cowboy, who cried out, dropped the gun, and fell back to the ground. Rachel aimed her revolver at the other cowboys. "You going to make me shoot all of you?" she asked incredulously. "I'm no expert, but you're all close enough to where that doesn't matter."

"Hold on—Hold on!" the leader beseeched again. "No need for that."

"I grew up around wild men, my brother included—only he was killed by men like you." With her Colt in one hand, she drew the Winchester from her saddle scabbard with the other. She aimed the rifle and returned the Colt to its holster. She spoke calmly. "Now, I will ask you just *one* more time."

—•—

That night, Ty and Jess, along with the other passengers on the moving train, were asleep. Two rows behind, in the moonlight through the window, Hamilton observed a tintype of Rachel and Matthew at their wedding. In the seat next to him, Elihu was in deep slumber, his head against the window. Hamilton stowed the photograph, leaned back, and closed his eyes.

At three in the morning, the conductor entered the car and strode down the aisle, heralding their arrival. "Lordsburg," he called out with sufficient voice to wake those sleeping. Then after a few more steps, "Lordsburg," he called out again.

—•—

In the darkness, Hamilton rode up to the Lordsburg marshal's office. A lantern light emanated from within. Hamilton dismounted and entered.

Inside, a man sat on the corner of Matthew's desk cleaning his revolver. He was in conversation with the banker, Ignatius Green, and did not take notice of Hamilton entering.

"I'm Hamilton Pierce," he interrupted.

At this, the man cleaning his gun came to attention, stood and holstered his weapon. "Thought you were someone else," he said as an apology. "I was expectin' the doc for a hurt prisoner I've got back there," he explained, motioning to a rear cell. "Yes sir. Got your message you were comin' in on the night train. I'm Carson Rain, acting marshal." He gestured to the man beside him. "This here's our banker, Ignatius Green. I woke him up so he could answer any questions on Matthew Donovan's estate."

Mr. Green nodded with a friendly smile.

"My daughter, Mr. Rain—when did she leave?"

"Yesterday, the mornin' after the funeral, Mr. Pierce. She has about a full day on you." He took his seat back on the desk. "She took Matthew's Winchester and the '62 Navy Colt she owned and rode east out of town—same direction as the men who shot Matthew down."

Hamilton turned to leave. "Much obliged."

Ignatius Green quickly stepped forward. "Mr. Pierce, I was instructed by Rachel to get a fair price for all holdings—land, horses, home, anything of value."

Hamilton took this in.

"Now, if you object, I can—"

"Mr. Green, I have no say in the matter. Please go forward with her wishes. I appreciate your time tonight." He turned again and left.

Hamilton emerged from the marshal's office. Outside were Ty, Elihu, and Jess on horses. Carson Rain and Ignatius Green followed him out.

Hamilton mounted.

The acting marshal leaned a hand against a post and regarded Hamilton. "Good luck to you, Mr. Pierce. We think the world of Rachel. If there's anything else we can do—"

"What happens now is up to us and Providence," Hamilton responded.

They spurred their horses east, out of town.

———◆———

Two hours later, in the early morning darkness, Hamilton and Ty observed from their horses the distant and dying campfire of four sleeping cowboys—the same four bronc busters Rachel had bested. Behind them, Elihu and Jess had dismounted and taken seat on a fallen tree, eating biscuits.

"Who do you think they are?" Hamilton asked.

His eyes on them, Ty said nothing.

"Any ideas?"

"Maybe them. Maybe not."

Annoyed, Hamilton swung his gaze to him. "If he could tap it out, my horse could have given me that answer." He turned his scrutiny back to the distant cowboys. After a moment, he glanced to Ty. "They wouldn't have a fire going if they were being hunted," he said, thinking it through.

"Maybe they don't know they're being hunted—or care," Ty countered.

After an extended silence, Hamilton fixed his eyes on Ty. "Twenty-five percent of my ranch will make you a wealthy man, but I'm coming up awful shy on my side."

"Well, here's an idea," Ty said, speaking up. "Why don't

you ride down there and introduce yourself. Inform them what a fine individual you are—being a former territorial governor and all—and if they shoot you, I might just get the idea that they're the men we're after."

Irritated, Hamilton turned his reins and stepped his horse over to Elihu and Jess. He was aware Ty knew no more than he did, but he was in no mood to be made sport of. "We're going in," he said to them. The two men jumped up and moved to mount their horses.

"Let's wake 'em up," Hamilton said to all.

———◆———

The bronc busters were stirred from deep sleep by horse hooves stepping all about the campsite. They were startled to discover Ty, Hamilton, Elihu, and Jess among them with rifles drawn on skittish horses, whose breaths billowed from their nostrils in the cold air.

The leader of the cowboys quickly got to his feet. "What the hell!"

Hamilton turned to Ty. "Are these the men?"

Ty sized them up. "No."

Two other bronc busters got to their feet—one slept on. The cowboys wrapped themselves in their blankets in the blustery cold as they tried to keep warm.

Hamilton spoke up. "My name is Hamilton Pierce. We're looking for four men. One, Juan de La Rosa; another, Tom Braden."

Ty caught movement of a rattler slithering into the bed-roll of the still-sleeping bronc buster some distance away, apparently escaping the cold and the commotion. He turned to the cowboys' leader. "Mister, a rattler just took sanctuary in that man's blanket."

The sleeping bronc buster began to arouse.

The leader hurried over and put a firm hand on his shoulder, pinning him down. "Don't move—don't even twitch," he said, with urgency filling his tone and manner. "Do you hear me?"

The sleepy cowboy, taken aback by the strength of his words and his hand, gawked at him in wonder. Finally, he sensed the movement in his blanket and froze in fear.

"What a' we do? What a' we do?" asked a fearful bronc buster.

"We'll smoke it out," the leader said. "Bring me a stick from the fire."

"Too slow—you'll spook it," Ty said.

The leader turned irritated eyes to Ty. "Then what the hell do you suggest?

"Shoot it."

The leader gave it a quick thought, nodded, and moved his hand to his holster.

"Could miss with that," Hamilton warned, and un-sheathed his Colt revolving shotgun from his saddle and tossed it to the leader, who stood and admired the rare gun for a moment.

Elihu and Jess readied their rifles as a warning to the now-armed man.

"That damn rattler won't know what hit him!" an excited bronc buster said.

The once-sleepy cowboy was perspiring from fear in spite of the cold morning. From the movement under the blanket, it was clear the rattler had curled up next to his leg.

The leader approached him with the shotgun. "Now . . . don't you worry, Billy. Just keep your leg real still." He stood over the blanket and aimed at the shape next to Billy's leg. He pulled the trigger. The muzzle blast from the powerful black powder gun obliterated the snake underneath, shattering the stillness of the morning and igniting the woolen blanket. The scared bronc buster quickly rolled away.

"Damn!" said one of the bronc busters, obviously amazed.

The leader stomped out the blaze. He turned his gaze to Hamilton, admired the weapon one more time, and presented it back to him. "Much obliged for the shotgun. We're horse breakers. Been picking up work at a ranch near here."

"As I said, we're looking for four men that passed through this way," Hamilton said.

"I'll tell you the same thing I told that woman who asked yesterday—"

"What woman?" Hamilton came back.

"Crazy woman!" interjected a bronc buster. "Pulled a Navy Colt on me before I could take a breath and struck me across my jaw," he said, motioning to the mark on his face.

"Shot my horse and my arm!" added another.

The leader sighed. "They didn't take her serious. Now I'm short a horse and got half a rider. Don't have much patience left, either—all because I ran into that woman. Damn her hide."

"Damn good horse, too!" the now-horseless bronc buster chipped in.

"She's my daughter."

At this, the leader pushed his hat up. "Well, I will tell you what I told her, Mr. Pierce. We crossed paths with those men she's after. They mentioned San Antone, and that was the direction they pointed their horses."

"Much obliged," Ty said.

The leader continued, "Look, some of us here may not be too smart, but we're generally law abidin'. Your daughter has some sand, but I took measure of those men and I wouldn't give her a water drop's chance in hell if she catches up with them."

Hearing what they needed to, Hamilton and Ty spurred out of camp with Elihu and Jess following.

The leader called after them. "This ain't good country for a woman alone."

CHAPTER SEVEN

A Rough Night in Mesilla

An unending gray sky stretched before Rachel as she approached a small town in the distance. A light snow fell, covering her hat and long coat. She tipped her hat down against the wind and cold. She soon passed a sign firmly planted on the outskirts that read Mesilla. The white landscape lay undisturbed in front of her, covering the trail of any earlier travelers coming and going that day. The solitary tracks she was leaving behind would soon be gone, too.

She walked her horse slowly down the street. She came upon a rectangular-shaped plaza, which represented the original settlement's defensive design against attacks from the Apache. Within this plaza, she passed an adobe blacksmith shop and a more modern brick mercantile building. The town was quiet. The weather was keeping the citizens at bay. There was little visible activity other than a few citizens hurrying along the boardwalks carrying out the necessities of the day, moving from one warm sanctuary to another. The saloons were quiet at this time of day, and it was a Monday.

Soon the words Mesilla Livery in old, weathered paint could be seen through the falling snow. She angled her horse over. A light emanated from within. She dismounted and led her horse in.

Within this sanctuary, Rachel paused to peer about. A few lanterns gave light. A young stablehand with a pitchfork was down a few stalls pitching manure. He gave little notice to her. She knocked the snow off and shook it from her hat. She then located an empty stall, led her horse in, and began to tend to her. As she removed the saddle, she heard muffled voices and looked over at the stablehand, who apparently didn't hear or was not concerned. She shrugged it off and tossed the saddle down. The muffled voices rose again. She peered around and located them coming from a darkened corner of the stables. Curious, she moved over to investigate. As she neared, she caught a glimpse of a burly man on top of a young woman. She quickly recognized the hurried movements and sounds of two people engaged in sexual activity.

"My apologies," Rachel said, as she turned and stepped away, moving back toward her stall. "Didn't mean to intrude." She glanced to the stablehand shoveling manure close by, who paid no attention to her or the goings-on she had witnessed. The smell of dung hung in the air. She shook her head and glanced back over her shoulder in the direction of the burly man. "Sure take your lady to nice places," she commented sarcastically, but not loud enough for him to hear—she thought.

"What the hell did you say?" came the burly man's angry voice, his words emerging from his hurried breathing and grunting.

"Just—go about your business," Rachel responded, tossing the words back over her shoulder. "I'm sure she just wants you to get it over with."

She heard a primal yell of anger.

Rachel whirled to see him leap up in fury. He pulled up the suspenders on his woolen, pin-striped trousers. The young woman quickly got to her feet and smoothed her dress, knocking away any dirt and hay, and fled the stables. The man stood with his button fly open. His member that had just offended the girl was exposed.

"I was having a good time with her," he said, his tone obscene.

The stablehand tossed one last pitch of hay and stopped to observe, his eyes growing wide.

The burly man looked Rachel up and down. "'Cause you interrupted me, I didn't get my money's worth—with her," he said, his words suggesting an alternative.

Rachel began to retreat.

He unsheathed a large knife from a scabbard on his waistband. "Looks like you're going to take her place," he said, smiling through his missing teeth. He rushed toward her.

Rachel reached for her revolver as she stepped back, trying to put distance between them. But before she could bring the gun to bear, he was upon her, and with a sweep of his arm, he violently knocked it out of her hand. Stumbling, she turned and attempted to run. He struck her, and she fell face first, hitting the ground hard. She rolled over to face him. He jumped on top of her and whooped in satisfaction.

Rachel struggled futilely against the man who loomed over her. He moved the point of the knife about her neck. "I am going to skin you good," he said, smiling obscenely. He thrust the tip of the knife into the ground next to her head. "That is—when I'm through with ya." He unbuttoned her long coat and threw it wide open. "Let's see what we got here," he said, looking her over. "You look a whole lot better than little Alice. Now, where did I leave off with her?" he asked himself. "Oh, yeah, I remember." With both hands, he violently ripped open her shirt. With a strong hand on her throat, he grabbed her trousers and began to yank them down.

The stablehand charged with the dung-covered pitchfork. "Get off!" he cried out as he thrust the manured tines, piercing the burly man just below his ribs. The impact knocked him to one side and off Rachel. He cried out in pain. She quickly rolled away. Firmly planted in the meat and fat of his body, the pitchfork stood fully erect. It swayed and wobbled with each pained breath from the unwanted penetration. With one strong arm, the burly man knocked it aside, tearing it away from his flesh.

The stablehand dashed to safety near the entrance.

Rachel scrambled for her saddle.

The burly man, with one hand on his wounds, hurried after her in pursuit. He shouted in rage.

She yanked her Winchester out of its scabbard, fell back against the stall, and fired into the charging man three times. He fell face first at her feet—dead before he hit the ground. Breathing heavy, she stared at him in disbelief.

Watching from the livery entrance, the wide-eyed stablehand ran over and fell to his knees next to her. "You all right, miss?"

"Yes." After a moment, she moved her gaze to the young man. "Thanks to you."

He turned his gaze to the dead man. "Oh, no," he managed to say, his breath collapsing. "What am I going to do now?" he asked vacantly, his words and manner full of fear.

"Don't worry," Rachel said, getting to her feet. "I can guarantee you he's dead," she added, holding the Winchester at her side.

The stablehand shook his head. "No," he said. "You don't understand." He lifted panicked eyes to her. "His brother is going to kill me! Ole Buck will do me in for sure!"

Just then, the Mesilla marshal, John Upchurch, a man of thirty-two years, and his young deputy, Rolfe Thompson, along with several townspeople, raced into the stables. The marshal and deputy had handguns drawn. They turned their weapons on Rachel when they saw the dead man.

"Drop that Winchester right now, or I'll shoot you dead—woman or not," the marshal warned.

Rachel let it drop. She felt the cold for the first time, pulled her ripped shirt together as best she could, and buttoned her long coat.

The deputy stepped over to the burly man lying face down and knelt to get a good look. "Looks like Big Mike," he said, identifying him. He rose, retrieved Rachel's Winchester, and stood, peering down at the dead man.

"Well, I'm waiting," the marshal said, his eyes on Rachel. "Just who in the hell are you, and just exactly what happened here?"

"I saw it all, marshal," the stablehand interjected quickly, the excitement of the events still with him. "He—he was assaulting her."

"Did you have a hand in the killing, Tommy?" the sheriff inquired.

The stablehand looked fearful. His lips were moving to answer the question but nothing was coming out.

"No," said Rachel, jumping in. "I'm responsible. He had nothing to do with it—I killed him," she said, looking down at the dead man.

The marshal turned back to her. "And just *who* are you?"

She lifted her eyes to him. "Rachel Donovan."

He peered at her for a moment, and then holstered his gun. "All right then, why don't you tell me what happened. Though I have a pretty good idea."

"I was just tending to my horse, intending to stay the night here in Mesilla, when he and I had some words and that son of a bitch pulled that knife," she said, motioning, "and jumped me."

The deputy stepped over and yanked the thrust knife from the ground, inspected it, and looked to the marshal. "That's Big Mike's skinner all right."

"I was determined not to let him use that on me—or anything *else* of his."

The deputy rolled Big Mike over. In doing so, he got some of the manure from the pitchfork on his hands. He wiped it off and caught sight of Big Mike's unbuttoned crotch with his manhood still exposed. He recoiled and turned away. "Marshal Upchurch," he said to get his attention.

The marshal turned his gaze to Big Mike and grimaced. "Christ sake! Throw something over his shame or turn 'im back over!"

The deputy rolled him back over.

"We've seen all we need to," the marshal said. "Tommy, finish tending to Mrs. Donovan's horse and go on home. Everyone else, go on about your business. Mrs. Donovan, you will need to come with me." He turned to the deputy. "Rolfe, get Doc Williams to make it official that he's dead, and get him over to the undertaker for burial in the morning." The deputy nodded, handed the Winchester to the marshal, and quickly left the livery. The marshal swung his eyes back to Rachel and motioned for her to follow.

The light snowfall and wind had stopped, leaving behind a cold calmness. Rachel and Marshal Upchurch moved across the plaza toward the jail. The saloons were now lively. The incident at the livery had stirred them up. The exterior of the town still appeared tranquil—the weather won that battle. But there had been a death—a man shot and killed—and those now-stimulated by such events weren't about to let that tranquility enter the saloons.

"Who was he, Marshal?" she asked.

"'Big Mike' McCloskey," he replied. "He owned a saloon with his brother over in Las Cruces. Ventured in now and then for the 'ladies.'"

"And Ole Buck?" she asked, repeating the name the scared stablehand had said.

The marshal turned to her evidently wondering how she had heard of him. "Tommy tell you about him?" he asked, reasoning it out.

Rachel nodded. "Just his name and that he was afraid of him."

"And for good reason—he's Big Mike's brother. He's the one you've got to be concerned about now. As mean—meaner in my opinion—than Big Mike back there. Whole family as lawless as they come." Focusing his thoughts, he continued, "Now here's the situation, Mrs. Donovan. Come mornin', the word will get to Ole Buck in Las Cruces, and he'll come looking for you. By tomorrow night, all hell will break loose here in Mesilla."

"How long are you going to hold me?"

"I'm not—officially. I want you to stay in the jail tonight for your own protection. Big Mike had some local friends, probably pretty liquored up by now, and wouldn't care that you're a woman. I'll stay in the jail with my deputy tonight to make sure of your safety. It's the least I can do." After a brief moment, he added, "You see . . . I knew your husband, Mrs. Donovan."

Taken aback, she paused in her tracks and peered at him. He turned back to face her.

"I met him in Wilcox when he was deputy there. I served along with him. It was before he met you," the marshal explained. "And you must now be tracking his killers—that's easy enough to figure out. But what I don't understand is why you're traveling alone."

"For now," Rachel responded. "My father, Hamilton Pierce, and the help he will bring from Arizona, are somewhere behind me. They'll catch up with me. But until then, I can't let these men disappear. I can't let their trail grow cold," she explained. "I'm capable enough to pursue them."

Marshal Upchurch nodded as he lifted his eyes back the way he and Rachel had come, back to the livery in the distance. "I can sure enough see that, Mrs. Donovan." He dropped his gaze back to her. "Is it from Matthew's teaching, if you don't mind me askin'?"

"My father's."

He motioned for them to continue. "Well, De La Rosa came through here yesterday. Had I known about Matthew then, my deputies and I could have tried to stop them. And since I didn't know you were pursuing him, it's safe to assume that neither do they—yet. Just remember, those men have friends most everywhere."

"Thank you, Marshal."

He halted in front of the old adobe jail. "But our concern tonight is Ole Buck. Self-defense or not, it ain't going to mean spit to him. If he catches you, he'll split you open from stem to stern like Big Mike had in mind. And he will do it right out here in the street."

"What about you, Marshal?" she asked. "Where will you be?"

"If it comes to that, Mrs. Donovan, you can be sure I'll already be dead."

———◆———

Dim and musty, the adobe jail held four cells, two up front and two in back. The deputy was seated at the desk in the corner. Leaning back in his chair, he had placed a boot atop the desk.

In a back cell, Rachel lay on the bed, her eyes to the ceiling in thought. Marshal Upchurch had returned her Winchester and it lay by her side, along with her holster and Navy Colt. She heard him entering the jail escorting two prisoners. She interrupted her thoughts to listen.

Up front, the marshal gave the two prisoners a shove. "Lock up our esteemed citizens: Hezekiah Pity and Jasbo Hester," he said to the deputy.

The deputy sighed deeply and got up from the chair, extracting himself from his comfortable position. "What's it this time?"

"Public indecency," Upchurch responded with an irritated tone. He gave them another shove toward their destination—the jail cells, as if they were local characters who had seen the inside of these types of accommodations many times.

The deputy took it from there and directed both the prisoners to a front cell, together.

"Had to chase these fine citizens across the plaza," the marshal informed him.

The deputy swung the iron door shut, locked it, and then returned and reassumed his resting position at the desk.

"Mabel had no call to take a broom to us, Marshal," Hezekiah said, his tone full of complaint.

"Yeah, she assaulted us!" accused Jasbo.

"You were relieving yourselves in her storage room," the marshal came back with a weariness in his words. He then swung his gaze to Rachel's cell in the back and moved toward it.

"It's a lie!" Hezekiah shot back. "Assault, plain and simple. We want to prefer charges."

"Shut up," came the marshal's quick response as he passed their cell. "And close your drawers," he added with exasperation, after a quick glance revealed Hezekiah's immodesty. "Christ! It seems to be the night I see everybody's open drawers."

Rachel heard him approach and turned her eyes toward him as he appeared outside her cell.

He pulled from his pocket a small sewing kit and extended it to her through the bars.

She sat up.

"Needle, thread, and some buttons to replace the ones you lost," he explained. "Got the owner to open up the general store."

She accepted them with a smile. "Thank you, again, Marshal."

"You'll have some privacy back here." He motioned to the two prisoners. "They can't see you."

"Is that a *female* I hear?" came Jasbo's voice.

Rachel lifted her eyes from the sewing kit. "Can you tell me anything about the men I'm after?"

He leaned a hand on a cell bar. "I believe they're headin' for San Antone. Other than De La Rosa, whom you're aware of, one's Tom Braden, and that is where he is from. He carries a hidden Bowie knife. I had him in jail here a few times for fightin'. Had to relieve him of it. As for the others they were with . . ." He momentarily cast his eyes aside in remembrance. "I've never seen them before."

Hezekiah's voice drifted back. "Marshal, she sounds *real* pretty."

"That's right," agreed Jasbo. "Like the *coo* of a dove," he added, his words dreamy.

Upchurch swung his eyes to them. "Shut up, the both of ya!" He returned his attention to Rachel. "I'll give you some privacy." He moved away.

In the shadows of the cell, Rachel removed her coat. She then took off her shirt and went to work with the needle and thread.

Up front, the marshal stowed the keys in the desk and took a seat on the corner of it.

The prisoners, their faces mashed up against the bars, angled a look back in Rachel's direction to no avail.

"Need someone to show you around town, Miss?" Jasbo asked in a hopeful lilt.

"Yeah, we wouldn't have run so hard to get away if we knew what was waiting for us here," added Hezekiah.

"We know all the places to get a free meal," Jasbo informed her. "They won't chase you away or nuthin'."

Annoyed, the deputy tipped his hat down over his face.

With his face pressed up against the bars, Jasbo looked to the marshal. "What's she in for?"

"Killed Big Mike," Upchurch responded simply, as he took in hand correspondence lying on top of the desk.

Jasbo and Hezekiah's eyes grew wide. They looked to one another, obviously taken aback, and turned their gaze back to the marshal.

"*Killed* Big Mike, you say," Hezekiah said.

"Damn!" Jasbo tossed in.

"Three shots with a .44 caliber Winchester at close range," Upchurch said absently, looking over the correspondence. "Tight pattern," he added, then lifted his eyes from the paperwork, apparently getting an idea on how to stop their annoyances. "And if you two don't stop being a nuisance to her, I'll make sure I release all of you at same time to give her a chance to chew things over with you."

"Oh, no-no," jumped in Jasbo. "That won't be necessary, Marshal." He swung his eyes back in Rachel's direction. "My apologies, ma'am."

Hezekiah nodded. "Yeah—that goes for me too, miss."

Upchurch lifted his eyes from the mail he held in front of him, as if getting another thought. He tapped his finger on the desk. After a moment, he put the papers aside, grabbed his Winchester, and moved to leave. "I'm going to take a look around," he informed the deputy.

The deputy nodded under his hat.

In a back cell, Rachel buttoned her now-mended shirt and lay back to rest. Weary, she went quickly to sleep.

———◆———

Sometime later, she was awakened by the two prisoners in conversation. They spoke softly to one another. She closed her eyes to go back to sleep.

"Did you hear what the marshal said?" she heard Jasbo ask. "She's after Mr. Braden," he stated, answering his own question.

"Mr. Braden was real nice to us, wasn't he?" she heard Hezekiah respond. "I bet he's livin' it up at The French House right now. What do you think, Jasbo?"

At this, Rachel's eyes opened as she was brought to attention.

"Yeah!" she heard Jasbo agree. "He told us some stories about that place, didn't he? If ever we were in San Antone, come on by, he'd say."

They soon quieted. After a few moments, Rachel closed her eyes once again and went to sleep.

At two in the morning, Upchurch was making his rounds. Light snow began to fall once again. He moved down the boardwalk. He braced himself against the encroaching cold as he passed a merchant's adobe store. The town was dark but for a few lit saloons. The cantinas were quieter now that some of their best customers had reached their money limit—or liquor limit—having passed out, not to awaken until late morning. The marshal heard the crunch of snow under quick, approaching footsteps and turned. A local man hurried up to him. They had a brief exchange. The local man went on his way, and Upchurch strode back toward the jail with purpose.

Rachel didn't hear the marshal enter the jail. Nor did she hear his hurried words with the deputy, who promptly left. Her deep sleep ignored his footsteps to her cell and his quick retort to "shut up" directed at the inquisitive Jasbo and Hezekiah. She was awakened, finally, by her cell door being opened. She turned her eyes to the marshal.

"It's best you go, Mrs. Donovan," Upchurch told her.

Clearing the cobwebs, she swung her legs to the side of the cot and peered up at him. "Why?"

"For your own safety," he explained. "My deputy will have your horse out front."

"I thought staying *here* was for my own safety?"

"Big Mike had a friend with him tonight from Las Cruces that I didn't figure on. He hightailed it back."

Rachel gathered her coat, holster, and Winchester.

"Thinkin' you might try to leave, Ole Buck could be here before first light—sooner, most likely."

The prisoners pressed themselves against the bars once again, waiting to get a glimpse of her. First came Upchurch and Rachel followed. Their eyes grew wide as the beautiful woman passed them.

"Well I'll be . . ." Jasbo said, his mouth staying open.

"And she was not more than ten feet from us," added Hezekiah. "Real nice meetin' you," he called after to her.

"A real pleasure," added Jasbo.

Rachel followed the wary marshal into the street. The snow was falling thicker now, gathering on whatever it could find. The deputy rode up with a sense of urgency, leading Rachel's horse. Rachel secured the Winchester in the saddle scabbard and mounted.

"Marshal Upchurch, I seem to be always thanking you—"

"Go on now and good luck to you, Mrs. Donovan," the marshal said. "You did what you had to, and I will do what I have to."

Rachel offered a smile of thanks and spurred her horse south out of Mesilla and into the darkness.

———◆———

Not long after, Ty, Hamilton, Elihu, and Jess walked their horses wearily into Mesilla. In the snowfall, they rode through the street, bracing themselves against the weather. Hamilton's eyes searched the town. They strode by the same adobe blacksmith shop Rachel had earlier. The town was quiet, but for a few still-lit saloons persisting into the late morning, accompanied by occasional drunken laughter. They soon passed the Mesilla Livery.

"I don't know what time it is, but it's late," Hamilton said. "We've been ridin' close to twenty-four hours. We need rest. Let's find a place to sleep, then stable these horses."

They rode up to the Mesilla Hotel. Through the falling snow, a light emanated from within the lobby. Elihu dismounted and moved to enter. The rest remained on their horses.

Elihu entered the hotel and closed the door behind him with a firm thud, which, along with the cold rush of air that followed him in, awoke the dozing night clerk, who was in a chair behind the register.

"Welcome to Mesilla," the clerk offered in greeting, getting to his feet and obviously struggling to shake off the sleep.

"How much for four men?"

"Two to a room. Three dollars a room," he responded, turning the register toward Elihu. "That'll make it six dollars, payable in advance."

Elihu pushed money, and signed in.

"Planning on staying long?" the clerk inquired.

"We're leaving in the morning."

"Even though it's a few hours before dawn, rate is the same, whether you stay all night or just a part of it."

Elihu nodded. Just then, gunshots were heard outside, somewhere in the distance. Elihu hurried out.

Outside the hotel, Ty, Hamilton, and Jess were alert. Elihu quickly mounted.

"Elihu, find out what it is and where it's comin' from," Hamilton ordered.

"Yes sir!" He turned to Jess. "Let's go." They spurred off.

Ty looked to Hamilton for instructions.

"Spooner, you go with them—in case there's trouble. I am going to the jail to talk with the marshal."

Ty spurred after Elihu and Jess.

Hamilton walked his horse toward the jail. He didn't want to attract attention. There was no need to hurry. They were there for the night. As he neared, he spotted a large man approaching the jail. He was bearded, and by his step and posture he appeared to be drunk and angry. Hamilton could see that the man carried in his hand an 1848 Colt Dragoon Cavalry revolver—what he knew to be a powerful .44 caliber gun. It was a large weapon often holstered on horses, rather than men, due to its size.

Cautiously, Hamilton rode up.

"Mister," the man spat out, his eyes on the jail, not Hamilton, "I'd git if I were you."

"Not looking for trouble, mister," Hamilton responded in an easy tone. "Just came here looking for my daughter."

The man stopped in his tracks in the snow and turned his attention to Hamilton. "What did ya say?"

Hamilton dismounted "Calm down, mister. I'm just here in town looking for my daughter." Hoping to avoid any possible trouble, Hamilton cut the conversation short, stepped past the drunken man, and moved toward the jail.

"And just *who is* your daughter?"

Hamilton continued on and did not look back. "Mister, that's none of your business."

"Rachel Donovan?" he inquired.

Hamilton stopped and turned. "Yeah. And just who in the *hell* are you?"

Before Hamilton could react, the man raised his Colt Dragoon revolver, leveling it at him.

Hamilton froze.

"Rachel Donovan is your daughter!" the man said, his voice rising in anger and disbelief.

Hamilton started to retreat. "Hold on, mister!"

Marshal Upchurch swung open the front door of the jail, gun in hand. "Buck!" he yelled, getting his attention away from Hamilton.

Ole Buck swung the large weapon in the marshal's direction, and both men fired simultaneously.

Hamilton drew his revolver.

Ole Buck's shot splintered the wood above the marshal's head. Upchurch's shot found its mark in Ole Buck's side just below the ribs. He recoiled in pain.

Hamilton fired, striking Ole Buck in the upper chest. Stepping back, Hamilton stumbled, sitting back into a water trough.

Ole Buck turned on Hamilton, firing the large caliber bullets, which tore gaping holes into the sides of the water trough, just missing Hamilton.

Hamilton and Marshal Upchurch continued firing, smoke mixing with the falling snow, dropping Ole Buck to his knees, and, finally, with no life left in him, he fell forward.

Hamilton stared at the dead man in disbelief. He pushed himself up and out of the cold water of the trough, water spouting from the bullet holes. As the snow fell around him, he stood, gun in hand and soaking wet, the excess water falling from his person. "What the *hell*!" he declared.

Ty, Elihu, and Jess rode up fast.

Hamilton took seat on the side of the trough. "How in the hell did that son of a bitch know my daughter? And just what in the hell was he so mad about?"

"You all right, Mr. Pierce?" Elihu asked.

The marshal swung his gaze to Hamilton. "Pierce?" he inquired, jumping in. "Mr. Hamilton Pierce?"

"That's right," Hamilton said.

Upchurch turned his attention to the deputy. "Rolfe, what about the gunfire we heard?"

"Ole Buck's boys creating a decoy for him," he responded. "Saw them scurrying out of town."

Hamilton shook his head in disbelief. He was angry at the senselessness of it. He motioned to the dead man. "All I did was inform that bastard I was looking for my daughter, and he leveled that Dragoon on me!" After a moment, he added, "This is why I left the Rangers! Between Comanches, Kickapoos, Mexicans, and desperadoes, I got tired as *hell* of being shot at!"

"Ole Buck here was after your daughter, Mr. Pierce," informed Upchurch. "She shot his brother dead."

Hamilton looked to the marshal. His thoughts shifted from himself to his daughter, the anger replaced by concern.

"It was self-defense," Upchurch explained. "Had her in my jail where she got about eight hours sleep. She left town about two hours ago on her rested horse." He then moved over to Ole Buck's body, knelt, and observed the dead man. "Up 'til tonight, he and his brother owned a cantina in Las Cruces. I suppose ownership will now go to someone who *actually* admits to being their kin." He rose to his feet. "Your daughter kind of left you the worst of it. That there was one of the meanest sons of bitches you'd ever meet, and you walked right into it. You're lucky to be alive—we both are."

At this, Ty turned his eyes to Hamilton and leaned forward on his saddle. "If we keep being 'introduced' to the 'friends' your daughter is making along the way, we're going to end up shot full of holes."

Hamilton swung his eyes to Ty—his blood still up. "What in the hell did you think this was!" he shot back. "Thought maybe you would just ride along, dazzle us with your company?! You're not running drunks out of your cantina here!" Hamilton paused and attempted to knock some of the wetness and anger off. "What the hell did you expect? You're well enough compensated."

"Had I known how *charmin'* she was, I'd have asked for more."

Hamilton started to respond when the undertaker moved in.

"I heard the commotion," the undertaker said to the marshal. He then began taking length and width measure of Ole Buck. "Looks like I'm not to get much sleep tonight. Just got through embalming Big Mike. Got to preserve him for transport back home to his family," he explained, and then shook his head as he took in the size of his next project that lay before him. "And now Ole Buck—and I'm runnin' low on formaldehyde. I'm expecting a delivery soon, though. For now, I'll just use what I have left with Ole Buck and add whiskey as a substitute to make up the difference. That should preserve him, along with putting them both out in the weather behind my store. So, it shouldn't be too unpleasant for the wagon driver transport-ing them both back to Las Cruces." He then riffled through Ole Buck's clothing. "Big Mike had no money on him. Alice was the recipient of what he did have when he arrived in town." He soon found some riches within a coat pocket and pocketed them. "This should cover the embalming costs for the both of them."

"Rolfe, help him get Ole Buck over to his furniture store," Upchurch instructed.

The deputy nodded, and he and the undertaker took an end, lifted the dead man, and began carrying him away.

Upchurch turned to Hamilton. "Our furniture maker doubles as our undertaker," he explained. "Making caskets is a good business for him."

Hamilton's heightened senses were calming. "That's the longest I stood listening to an undertaker go on about his business." He turned back to Ty. "We're making time on

Rachel, but we need rest, and so do our horses." He moved back to his horse. "All we can do is hope something slows her down between here and El Paso. She'll take the train from there to San Antone." He mounted and gathered reins. He glanced to his overall wetness and then to Ole Buck being conveyed toward the lantern-lit business down the street. "Me and that dead son of a bitch are about to freeze solid. But I'm still movin' in my wet clothes. Let's hurry up, stable these horses, and get to that hotel."

CHAPTER EIGHT

Ghosts of Fort Fillmore

The snow had stopped falling, leaving only the cold wind against Rachel's face. In the distance she could see the outline of an army fort against the night sky. She knew it meant sanctuary and the possible offering of warm food from those garrisoned there. She spurred her horse.

As Rachel neared, she pulled up as the sight became clearer. In the near distance, she now realized that what she had seen were only the remnants of an abandoned, adobe-walled outpost. She peered at it, her brow furrowed. It wasn't going to be the sanctuary she hoped, but it still meant a refuge from the wind. She urged her horse forward.

Rachel walked her horse through what was once the fort's front gate. A few steps in she pulled reins and paused to look about at the former garrison's interior. The clouds cleared and moonlight reflected off the snow that blanketed the ground. It all looked as cold as she felt, she thought. Many of the adobe structures were destroyed; only a few remained intact. Whatever was comprised of wood had been burned, the charred timbers gleaming in the moonlight. The original purpose of the buildings was now lost. Chimney silhouettes stood in erect salute as if in military review from long ago. She stepped her horse toward one of the clay brick buildings along the south wall for possible sanctuary for the remainder of the night. Her horse's footfalls on the fallen snow were the only sound.

She stopped her horse in front of the structure, looked it over for a moment, then proceeded to dismount. She stepped about the building, giving scrutiny to it. The sunbaked mud that had faced the fort's conflagration was scorched. She peered inside the entrance, and then took a step inside the dark interior. Thinking better of it, she stepped back out.

"Jolie," she said, taking her horse's reins, "I think it's best we make ourselves at home outside."

She led her horse to the leeward side of the sturdy structure. Out of the wind, she tied off her horse and took in her surroundings. "Looks like this is going to be our accommodations for the night," she said, satisfied. "I'll start a fire."

Rachel walked about the interior of the fort, collecting tinder and wood that wasn't already charred. The snow crunched underneath her boots. She paused and took a deliberate breath as she looked about at the ghostly ruins.

She listened to the silence that was all around. She wondered about the fort's purpose and why it was set ablaze. She wondered of the men who served and of those who died here. Coming out of her thoughts, she leaned down and retrieved more wood.

She returned to her shelter, dumped the wood up against the adobe building, and headed into the fort's interior once again. She stepped back through the fort's entrance, moving out into the exterior of the fort toward a stand of trees. Stepping through the snow, she collected what fallen limbs she could find. As she caught sight of a good piece of fire wood and bent down to retrieve it, she took notice of wolves howling in the distant darkness.

She returned to the clay brick structure and tossed the wood down in the growing pile she had pressed up against the adobe.

"One more trip should do it," she said to herself.

She heard the wolves howl once again.

This time she unsheathed her Winchester from her saddle before setting out.

With the all the wood collected she figured she would need, she leaned her Winchester against the structure near where she was going to start a fire. She cleared the snow from a small area and placed some of the collected wood in the center. Retrieving a tinder box from the saddle bags, she set to work starting a fire. From the box she removed bits of tinder she had gathered along the trail and placed them underneath the gathered wood. She peered back inside the tinder box. Inside were matches, and a piece of flint as the option of last resort. The hard gray rock was sewn into a leather cover to improve the grip on it. She pulled out a match.

Before long, the fire was going to her satisfaction. She untied and removed her blanket roll from the saddle and placed the blanket by the fire. She then unsaddled her horse, and finally plunked down against the clay brick, covering herself with the blanket. The firelight played off the colors of her horse, which contrasted against the surrounding shades of darkness, the limited hues of gray and black. She could feel the life-giving warmth as she peered into the fire. Soon her eyes moved from the growing, crackling flames to the ghostly ruins around her and its somber shadows. She heard the wolves howl again—closer this time. But they were to be kept at bay by the fire. After a moment, she leaned her head back against the structure, closed her eyes, and went to sleep.

She was awakened by the tell-tale sound of movement through the snow not far away. The blanket of white acted like a sentinel, alerting her to a presence. The fire crackled before her. She looked around, not sure if what she had heard was real or part of a dream. She could feel the cold at the outskirts of the flames. It further awakened her, and more wood was tossed onto the fire. She turned her gaze toward the darkened interior of the fort. All was quiet and still. Suddenly, she caught sight of a small shadowed figure darting across the snow. She reached for her Winchester. She then saw a taller silhouette, but this time she could make it out. It appeared to be an Indian woman stepping through the snow. Her posture was bent—she seemed forlorn. The image was quickly gone, disappearing behind an obstruction. With Winchester in hand, Rachel silently got to her feet and moved toward the fort's interior grounds, toward what she had seen.

Alert, she carefully stepped through the snow. She paused to look about, her rifle at the ready. Just then, she saw two more small shadowy figures darting across the snowy ground. She could make them out more clearly now. They were children—also Indian. Rachel heard their childlike laughter. But they, too, quickly passed back into the darkened shadows. She stared after them with disbelief. Just then, in her periphery, she caught movement. She swung her gaze and Winchester to the dark figures of two Indian women walking together, their heads down, trudging through the snow. She lowered her rifle. The two were oblivious to her. She knew from the outline of their dress that they were Apache.

"That just can't be," she said to herself disbelievingly.

She watched the two women move into the dimness and obscurity of the moonlit fort and then they were gone. Rachel looked around for more figures as she retreated, stepping slowly back toward the adobe structure and her fire, her eyes sweeping the fort. All was quiet and still again. As she neared the building, she turned and moved toward her warm sanctuary. Suddenly, two moonlit soldiers emerged from the darkness and shadow of a nearby building. She swung her Winchester. They stopped in their tracks.

"Company B, First Dragoons, ma'am," one said in identification. "We're sorry to startle you. I'm Private Dwyer, and this is Private Henning," he said with a head nod. "We're bivouacked nearby," he added, motioning to the south.

Private Henning nodded. "We were on sentry and saw your fire," he explained. "We're here to protect you, ma'am."

Rachel relaxed her stance, but kept the rife pointed in their direction.

"Captain Stanton allowed us to check on you," Private Henning continued. He lowered his gaze to her Winchester. "Is everything all right, ma'am?"

She glanced back toward the interior of the fort. "I—I believe I saw something moving within the shadows," she said simply, unwilling to divulge what she was beginning to think was all in her mind.

Private Dwyer spoke up. "That fire of yours sure looks warm, ma'am." He smiled. "We've been on the cold ground for a while."

She looked to the men and their shouldered rifles. She knew they could have harmed her already if they had wanted to. She motioned them to join her. "I'm glad to have the company."

She leaned her Winchester back against the adobe building and retook her seat against it. The soldiers unshouldered their weapons and sat on the other side of the fire.

In the firelight, she took notice of their antebellum guns. "My father collects guns. I believe I've seen one of those. Is that a Musketoon?"

"Yes, ma'am, it is," Private Henning responded, and took the weapon in hand. "A Springfield Model 1847," he said, with pride in his words. "Buck and Ball cartridge, .69 caliber."

"Those guns look a little dated to still be in service," she said.

"Standard issue, ma'am."

She accepted this and leaned back to rest.

"The First Dragoons used to be garrisoned here at the fort," Private Dwyer informed her. "As a matter of fact, you're leanin' against the very quarters where Captain Stanton and his wife lived."

"Well, I wasn't sure what had taken residence since," she responded, "so I felt safer out here."

Private Dwyer nodded in agreement. "Yes, ma'am."

"There are a lot of dangers out here, too," Private Henning stated.

"Hungry wolves, for one," added Private Dwyer.

"You heard them, too?" she asked. "Like I said—I'm glad you're here." She dropped her gaze to the fire.

"You said you saw shadows," Private Henning began. "Could they have been Apache women and children?"

"Yes!" she responded, lifting her gaze to them, amazed that they had asked, her self-doubts removed.

"Those Chiricahua spirits have been seen here before," said Private Dwyer.

"Chiricahua?" she inquired, thinking he was mistaken. "But wasn't this area inhabited by the Mescalero?"

Private Henning nodded. "After an Indian agent was killed by the Chiricahua back in '57, Colonel Bonneville led an expedition from this fort to the Gila River to take revenge. It was at the beginning of the Chiricahua Apache Wars. Over thirty Apache women and children were taken prisoner during the Battle of Turnbull Mountain. The Chiricahua captives were brought all the way back here to Fort Fillmore. Nine of the women and children died imprisoned in the guardhouse," he said, glancing to the interior, apparently in the direction of the former guardhouse.

"They're buried in the fort cemetery just south of here," added Private Dwyer. "Perhaps they are who you saw."

She nodded in thought, and lowered her gaze to the fire. After a moment, she lifted her eyes to the howls of nearby wolves.

"Don't you worry about them wolves, ma'am," Private Henning said reassuringly.

She then leaned back and closed her eyes.

She woke up abruptly sometime later. The two soldiers were still there, unmoving, staring into the flames. More wood had been placed on the fire to keep the cold and wolves at bay. Light snow had begun to fall once again, collecting on her blanket. She relaxed fully, pulled her blanket up, and drifted off into a deep sleep.

She awoke with the early morning light to a fresh, glimmering snowfall from the night before. The soldiers were gone. The fire was going out. The supply of firewood next to her was exhausted—fully utilized by the soldiers, who had kept her and themselves warm and kept the wolves at a distance. She arose and shook out her blanket. Her eyes followed fresh tracks in the snow, revealing the two young men had left not long ago in the direction they had come. She looked to the interior grounds of the fort, where the whiteout had erased all evidence of her presence. She rolled her bedroll, grabbed her Winchester and saddle, and moved to her horse.

She swung up into the saddle. Before her was a portion of the fort's south palisade that had fallen some years back. A white landscape and El Paso lay beyond. She gave a light spur. Once outside, a light flurry began to swirl and fall. She braced herself against the chill and urged her horse forward into the snowy New Mexico Territory landscape, leaving deep tracks. Back at her makeshift shelter, snowflakes began to collect within the shallow footfalls she and the soldiers left behind early in the morning. Soon all traces of their presence at the fort the night before would be gone.

CHAPTER NINE

The Acme Saloon
and the 1884 Election

Hamilton pulled up as he spotted the remnants of the old fort ahead. In better light, the condition of ruin and abandonment were better seen. "Maybe Rachel found shelter there last night," he said to the others, and they spurred their horses.

They trotted through the front gate and paused to look around at the snowy grounds.

"Fort Fillmore," Hamilton said, informing them. "Or— what's left of it."

"Who destroyed it?" Elihu asked.

"The Union army did," Hamilton stated. "After an unsuccessful attack on the Confederates at Mesilla, they blew up their supplies, set the fort afire, and abandoned it," he explained for Elihu and Jess's benefit. He knew Ty was aware of the fort and its history. "It was first established in the early '50s as part of a network of forts built to give protection to the western migration of settlers and traders. The area was beleaguered by Apache attacks. Many are buried here—both soldier and civilian."

"You sure know a lot about it, Mr. Pierce," Jess stated.

"I visited Fort Fillmore in '68," he explained, "when I accompanied representatives from Fort Selden north of here. Conditions at the Fort Fillmore cemetery had deteriorated badly since the Civil War. We came upon Captain Henry Stanton's grave in the cemetery just south of the post.

"Is he the namesake for Fort Stanton northeast of here?" Elihu asked.

"That's right," Hamilton responded. "He commanded Company B, First Dragoons out of Fort Fillmore. He was ordered to chase and kill whatever Apache Indian he could find. He was with his command pursuing the Mescalero up in the Sacramento Mountains east of here when he was killed along with two dragoon privates—Dwyer and Henning. By the time his command was able to recover their bodies, they found them full of arrows and half-eaten by wolves and turkey buzzards," he recounted. "They said it was a gruesome sight," he added, after a moment's reflection of that time. "That was almost thirty years ago." He took a deep breath, taking in the memory of those days. "The soldiers built a bonfire and burned away the flesh of those men. They took only the bones back here to Fort Fillmore. Anyway, we decided to move Captain Stanton's remains to the cemetery at Fort Selden."

"What about the two privates?" Jess asked.

"They remained here. The graves of Dwyer and Henning could not be identified," Hamilton explained. "There must have been seventy graves out there, and Stanton's was the only one with a marker—unfortunately. So those two soldiers are still out there in that cemetery, lying in that cold ground somewhere." He turned the reins, and stepped his horse away. "See if you can find some evidence of Rachel being here," he said, calling back.

Elihu and Jess urged their horses forward to look around. Ty set off in another direction.

Hamilton's horse stepped through the snow, its footfalls prominent in the morning stillness. He peered about. He soon paused before the burned-out remains of a building. He sat up straight in his saddle, taking a deep breath, and stretching his back. He took in the remnants for a moment as if it stirred a memory, and announced for all to hear, "George Pickett served here before the war—before his fateful charge at Gettysburg." He then quieted. "That's one blood bath I'm glad our Texas Brigade was not involved," he said to himself,

"Over here," Hamilton heard Elihu call out. He turned his horse and dug spur.

Soon Hamilton stepped his horse through the remnants of Rachel's fire from the previous night, set close to the adobe brick building. Elihu and Jess had dismounted and were looking about. Hamilton peered at the old structure from which Rachel had taken sanctuary from the wind.

"Officer's quarters," he said, identifying it. She probably didn't trust the inside." He looked around. "Her accommodations were not as nice as ours last night, but at least she was warm." He lifted his eyes to ghostly tracks leaving the fort through the section of perimeter wall that no longer stood. His gaze followed the indentations that left a suggestion of a trail that led south before disappearing, the hoofprints vanishing into the undulating white vastness.

"She's got a couple of hours on us," Ty said.

"Let's see if we can catch her in El Paso," Hamilton responded, spurring his horse. Ty followed. Elihu and Jess quickly mounted and hurried to catch up.

They came over a rise and pulled reins to stop and observe. In their sight was a large town.

Jess whooped. "Would you look at that, Elihu! El Paso, by God!"

"I never thought I'd see it," Elihu responded in awe, and then turned to Hamilton. "Think she's there, Mr. Pierce?" he asked. "Do you think we got here in time?"

Hamilton offered a sigh that didn't offer much hope. "Not unless Lady Luck plops right down on my lap, smiles, and favors me with her perfumed ample bosom," he said. "But she has favored me in the past," he added, and spurred. "Let's find out."

They sauntered their horses down the middle of the street.

There was much activity. All about were red-white-and-blue streamers, flags, bunting, and other colorful festive decorations. Bands could be heard playing off in the distance. Citizens strolled about attired in their finest, taking in the sights, or standing about immersed in conversation.

Elihu and Jess looked to one another with curiosity.

"What's goin' on, Mr. Pierce?" Elihu asked.

"It's Election Day," he responded vigorously. "November 4th. I had lost track of days." He peered around. "Our sacred right to vote—to choose our next president—all wrapped up in a gawd-awful spectacle."

All about them were men and women in campaign hats passing out flyers for their candidate, Democrat Grover Cleveland out of New York, while others did so for James G. Blaine, a Republican out of Maine. One attempted to pass a flyer to Hamilton, who declined, but found better luck with Jess, who took it in hand.

"If you've been readin' the papers," Hamilton continued, "this campaign has been marred by much political acrimony and personal invective. The issue of personal character of both candidates has marked this 1884 election." Though he was once a politician, Hamilton shook his head at the scene before him.

They soon rode past a group of Democrats, men and women, handing out leaflets and singing praises for their candidate Grover Cleveland. A male supporter stepped out to speak with Hamilton.

"I do so hope you're in town to support our candidate, the honorable Grover Cleveland," he said in a hopeful manner. "And not that rapscallion Blaine," he added, with distaste.

Hamilton dropped his gaze to the man and paused his horse. He decided to have sport with him. "I understand Mr. Blaine to be a senator. It is a noble calling," he said with seriousness.

"But sir," the man responded, obviously taken aback. "If you're not aware, letters have been found belonging to Mr. Blaine indicating he had sold his influence in Congress to various businesses. One such letter ended with the directive to 'Burn this letter.'"

The Democratic supporters holding signs behind the man began to chant:

Blaine, Blain, James G. Blaine
The continental liar from the state of Maine
Burn this letter!

A female supporter stepped out to join her fellow enthusiast in pleading their case to Hamilton. "Please cast your vote for the venerable Mr. Cleveland," she beseeched, "and not that corrupt and detestable Mr. Blaine."

Hamilton took a breath. "Well, I'll tell ya . . ." he began. "I understand your candidate Mr. Cleveland didn't do his own fightin' in the great Civil War. He, in fact, paid a substitute 150 dollars to take his place. It was a man by the name of George Benninsky, I believe—a thirty-two year-old Polish immigrant. It's interesting to note that Mr. Benninsky survived the war because nobody wanted to shoot him. Not a scratch. When someone had a bead on him, they'd say, 'Nope. A substitute just won't do. If I can't shoot Cleveland himself, why bother.'"

"Well!" exclaimed the female supporter, obviously incensed.

Hamilton continued. "I figure a man that lucky must be destined for something great—Mr. George Benninsky, that is," he added.

"*You* must be a Republican, sir! We have wasted our time!" the male supporter exclaimed.

"We don't think much of Mr. Blaine around here," she added. "Or Mr. Lincoln!"

Hamilton tipped his hat courteously. "Yes ma'am." He gave a soft spur, and the four riders moved on. Evidently angry at their very presence, the female supporter glared at each one as they sauntered past.

The four men soon approached an intersection and pulled up, yielding to a mule-drawn trolley passing by filled with cheerful and celebratory passengers. Two young female travelers gazed at Elihu and Jess and smiled. Elihu and Jess returned the smiles and tipped their hats. The trolley moved on with the two men looking after the two young women who still had eyes on them and talking excitedly to one another.

Hamilton spurred his horse forward once again, as did the others.

"Where are we going, Mr. Pierce?" Elihu asked.

"The Grand Central Hotel" Hamilton announced. "The largest hotel in Texas," he added as if it were a matter of pride. The trolley they had yielded to continued on—its fading celebratory conversation and laughter trailed back to them, finally dissipating into the broad festal atmosphere all around.

Hamilton looked about, taking it all in. "El Paso has developed a reputation for being a 'Sin City,'" he informed Elihu and Jess. He glanced back to Ty. "Mr. Spooner, here, has in the past helped to contribute to that dubious moniker. As a frequent visitor, he helped nudge this town and its citizens away from good standing."

Ty ignored him, keeping his eyes forward.

"We've heard of it being so, but I sure don't see the reasons, right off," Elihu said.

"You've only seen some of it," Hamilton came back. "There are saloons on almost every block, and you'll find gambling halls and a sprawling tenderloin district along Utah Street."

"Tenderloin district?" Jess inquired.

"Brothels," Elihu informed him.

"And there's opium dens," Hamilton added. "True *hell* holes," he followed up, the words spoken with feeling. "They were introduced by the Chinese who arrived with the railroad crews."

"Damn," Jess exclaimed.

Hamilton filled his lungs and looked about. "Yep—Sin City. Why, there wasn't even a church here of any kind until three years ago."

Elihu looked to Hamilton with a furrowed brow, his expression incredulous.

"With you boys being good Catholics," Hamilton continued, "I know you find that hard to believe. It's a woeful tale, but the Christian Church had no desire to build one here. The story goes—they were too afraid Mr. Spooner would return. They knew they were licked."

Elihu and Jess looked to one another, amused. They glanced to Ty, who had his gaze elsewhere as if he knew he was, once again, being made sport of by Hamilton.

"To tell you the truth," Hamilton continued, "they didn't put two boards together, or hammer one nail, to that Godly cause of constructing a house of worship until they heard he had fled to Mexico, hiding—ironically—in a cantina named 'Paradise.'"

Elihu smiled broadly and lifted his gaze to a three-story structure up ahead. It was painted white and had red-white-and-blue gala banners hanging from the windows and from the awning over the porch that stretched from one end to the other.

"Is that the Grand Central?" Elihu asked.

"She's pretty, isn't she," Hamilton said, answering his question. "She's quite a lady. Julia and I have taken a room there many times passing through. I have many fond memories."

Out front were Republicans handing out their circulars and singing praises for their candidate James G. Blaine, while at the same time denouncing Grover Cleveland and chanting:

Ma, Ma, where's my Pa?
Ma, Ma, where's my Pa?

They dismounted and moved to enter the hotel. A man wearing a Blaine for President hat descended on them as they stepped up onto the porch.

"Are you gentlemen in town to vote?" the Republican campaigner asked.

Elihu and Jess ignored him and entered the hotel.

"Nope," Ty said.

The Republican campaigner was taken aback. "You *must* know that it's presidential Election Day. And I would be grateful for your time to vote for our candidate, the esteemed and venerable James G. Blaine."

Ty continued past him. "No time to vote," he said, following Elihu and Jess inside.

Taken aback, the Republican campaigner called after him, "Everyone should make time to do their duty as an American citizen." He turned back and intercepted Hamilton. "How about you, sir?" he asked. "I do hope you are in town to support our Republican candidate, the esteemed James G. Blaine, and not that detestable Democrat, Grover Cleveland."

Hamilton peered at the man. "What's your name?"

"Melvin Turley, sir."

"Well, Mr. Turley, isn't that Cleveland fellow known as 'Grover the Good'?" he asked. "A moniker earned for his personal integrity?"

Obviously beside himself, the man responded, "But sir, we have found refutations from the past."

Hamilton looked to those chanting and holding signs. "What is that they're chanting?" he inquired.

"'Ma, Ma, where's my Pa?'" the campaigner answered with a smile, obviously proud of the slogan's creativity and effectiveness. "As we speak, sermons are being delivered from the pulpit across the country condemning Cleveland for fathering an illegitimate child while he was a lawyer in New York," he said, delighted to inform Hamilton of the misdeed. "Confronted with the scandal, Mr. Cleveland has admitted to paying child support to this woman."

Hamilton looked hard at the man. "Well, we now know Mr. Cleveland's failings. Now why don't you tell me the accomplishments of this man 'Blaine' for whom you want me to cast vote, one of our country's most sacred rights."

"Well—"

"Is he a good man? A fearless man? A man with vision for the country?"

Momentarily flustered by Hamilton's forceful, direct questions, the campaigner stammered. "Why, uh . . . yes."

Hamilton strode past him. "Mr. Turley, if you're not convinced, neither am I." He entered the hotel, leaving the befuddled Republican campaigner staring after him, his mouth open.

Hamilton closed the door on the scene outside and saw Ty standing in the middle of the lobby waiting on him. Elihu and Jess were at the front desk. Hamilton strode toward Ty.

"Did you enjoy yourself out there?" Ty asked.

"Politicians," Hamilton said, offering a snort of derision. "It's the one design flaw of this great country and this wonderful day. If we just didn't have to vote for politicians, we'd all be better off."

On a lobby couch, Levi Burch, a robust man of obvious success by his dress and manner, looked up from his paper. "Hamilton!" he exclaimed. "Hamilton Pierce!" He cast the paper aside, sprang up from the couch, and strode over.

"Real good to see ya, Levi," Hamilton said. He cast an eye to Ty. "This here is Mr. Spooner."

Levi nodded to Ty in greeting.

Elihu and Jess strode up.

"Got us two rooms," Elihu announced.

"And this is Elihu Merritt, my ranch foreman, and Jess Whitt, who works for me on the ranch. A good hand," he added. "This here is Levi Burch, an old friend of mine." Hamilton's gaze stayed on Levi. "Did you get my wire?"

He nodded. "The four men you spoke of arrived early yesterday. As per your instructions, I did not contact Sheriff O'Brien, but I don't know why. He's a good man."

"I had that in mind. I didn't want anyone else shot up before I got here."

"They were joined by a young fella off the train and two rough lookin' men—local outlaws, I believe—who arrived on horseback. Three left on the early morning train; four stayed, including that young fellow. They lived it up pretty good over at the Acme Saloon."

"Where are they now?"

"Still there. I have a fellow keeping an eye out. They're playing poker." Levi paused momentarily and added, "I don't know if you're aware of this, but from their liquor talk, they're waiting on you."

Hamilton looked at him questioningly.

"They were calling you by name—you and Mr. Spooner here."

Hamilton and Ty glanced to one another.

"When's the next train to San Antonio?" Hamilton asked, his eyes back on Levi.

"Just missed it by a few hours. Why?"

"Rachel was on that train," Hamilton informed him.

"Damn, Hamilton. If I'd known—"

"I couldn't take the chance on the telegraph clerk alerting De La Rosa. When's the next one out?"

"Not till mornin'. I'd sure like to know what's going on."

"Let's have dinner tonight, and I'll fill you in."

"My house then, six o'clock," Levi said briskly, adjourning the matter until then. He strode away toward the entrance. Half-way there he turned and added "Ole Cleveland is trying to get elected. The first Democrat in thirty years—not since Buchanan in '56," he said, obviously stimulated. "He will if Texas has anything to say about it." With a hearty laugh, he turned and moved away.

"We'll see you later, Levi," Hamilton said, calling after him.

At this, Levi paused at the hotel entrance. With his hand on the doorknob, he turned back to Hamilton. "Sarah will be setting the table for six," he said, with seriousness. "I'm hopin' that count will stand. She'll be disappointed if you . . . don't show."

"It'll disappoint some—others not so much. You give Sarah my best, ya hear."

With that, Levi grinned and exited.

"I'll take Elihu in with me," said Ty. "You and Jess back us up."

"No," Hamilton said firmly. "You and I are going in."

Ty shook his head. "As he said, they know we're coming. Some of those men could have spent time in Arizona Territory. And you've had your face on too many campaign posters in the past. They may have a harder time recognizing me—that wanted poster you spread around years ago was a poor likeness."

"What's the matter? Wasn't it pretty enough for ya?" Hamilton shot back. He then sighed, knowing Ty was right, and gave in. "All right, Jess and I will back you two up. I'll pick up Sheriff O'Brien."

"Elihu, you're with me," Ty said and moved toward the exit. Elihu followed.

The two men soon walked their horses up to the Acme Saloon. It was constructed of adobe and wood and sat on a corner across a wide street. Ty and Elihu dismounted. Piano playing and laughter emanated from within the saloon. Elihu drew his Winchester that slung from his scabbard.

Ty shook it off. "Might draw too much attention."

Elihu sheathed it and followed Ty inside.

The men moved to the bar, passing a table near the swinging doors where sat one of the outlaws that had stood with Juan de La Rosa that morning in Lordsburg. He sat drinking with two prostitutes, unaware of the identity of the men who just stepped past.

They reached the bar, and Elihu motioned to the bartender. "Two whiskies."

Leaning on the bar, Ty casually looked over his shoulder to look around. Tables were occupied with cowboys, whores, and some well-thought-of-citizens playing faro and poker. In the far corner, near a front window, was a four-chair table of poker. At the table facing them with cards in his hands was Seth Garrett, the former Pierce Ranch hand. Nearest the window was one of the local outlaws that came in on horseback. Another chair was filled by the local citizen Levi had asked to furtively keep an eye on them. The fourth chair was empty, the man having apparently stepped away momentarily, for his stakes were visible on the table. Ty brought his eyes forward and motioned Elihu to the corner table.

Elihu glanced over Ty's shoulder. "That's Seth Garrett," he quickly said in a low voice with disbelief. "He must have been the one off the train Mr. Burch spoke of. No wonder they knew we were comin'," he added, "If Seth loses interest in his cards, he's going to look up and recognize us."

Ty nodded.

"The only reason he's here is to sell us out," Elihu said, thinking it through, his voice tinged with anger. "I wonder how much money he got?" he asked with disdain.

"Whatever it was, he's using some or all of it as stake in that poker game," Ty said.

"De La Rosa must know everything about us now," Elihu stated. He stole a look at the whole of the saloon. "Which ones are the other three waitin' on us?"

Ty's eyes, hard and unwavering, locked with his. "Let's find out. Stay here," he said firmly. "Be ready." He pushed away and moved toward the poker table.

Seth received two cards from the dealer. He grimaced and tossed in his hand. He grabbed his beer, took a drink, and lifted his eyes to the man approaching their table. Seeing Ty, his eyes grew wide.

By the swinging doors, the Lordsburg outlaw's attention moved from the prostitutes to Ty. He took notice of Seth's response. Underneath the table, he smoothly pulled his gun and rested it on his lap. One of the girls laughed and playfully stroked the gun with her hand.

Seth jumped up from the table, spilling beer and poker chips, and reached for his holster. "Spooner, by God!"

Ty held up his hand. "No! That's not what I want!"

Seth cleared leather.

Ty quickly drew his .44 caliber and fired into the upper arm of Seth, knocking the gun from his hand and spinning him back against the wall. Seth cried out and sank to the floor. The outlaw by the window jumped up from the table and drew. Ty fired into his body. The wounded outlaw reflexively fired down into the table, its muzzle just above his stake, setting the paper money on fire and exploding his chips. He staggered back toward the window. Ty fired again, blowing him through the glass and onto the boardwalk. The townspeople outside the window cried out and scurried for safety. The local citizen at the table quickly threw his hands up, his eyes wide with fright.

The Lordsburg outlaw by the swinging doors jumped up from his table, gun in hand, and quickly fired at Ty, missing. He turned his gun on Elihu and fired, nicking his arm and exploding the whiskey bottle on the bar behind him. Elihu fired back, hitting him in the shoulder, spinning him. The prostitutes screamed and ran. The Lordsburg outlaw dashed for the saloon door.

Ty spun and fired, hitting him.

Elihu fired again, the bullet finding its mark. Mortally wounded, the outlaw stumbled forward and pushed through the swinging doors to escape. A shotgun blast was heard from outside and he was blown back through the swinging doors, dying before he landed onto the wood floor inside. As the shattered doors swung, Hamilton could be seen in the street with his 1855 Colt revolving shotgun, smoke billowing from its barrel.

Down the street, the other outlaw, who had come in by horseback and was the missing fourth man at the table, emerged from a nearby restaurant with a tray of food. He paused at the sound of gunfire from the Acme Saloon. Tossing the tray aside, he pulled a Winchester from a nearby horse and fired repeatedly at Hamilton, Jess, and Sheriff O'Brien. Jess was knocked off his feet. Hit in the heart, he died instantly. Hamilton dropped the shotgun— the distance too great—and drew his revolver and fired. Sheriff O'Brien returned fire with his handgun.

The outlaw moved toward the two men firing the Winchester, his firepower overwhelming the two men.

Inside the saloon, Ty fired through the shattered window into the street, hitting the outlaw, staggering him. Ty fired again. The outlaw dropped the Winchester and crumpled to the ground.

With his hands held high, the local citizen at the poker table peered up at Ty with fear in his eyes. "Son of a bitch, mister, I was just playing cards with them. I was asked to do so by a friend of mine who wanted me to keep an eye on them. If they owe you money—take it!"

"No, they don't owe me money," Ty responded, annoyed. He turned to Elihu. "You all right?"

"Nicked arm is all."

Ty moved to the shattered saloon window and peered out. "The sheriff is coming in," he informed Elihu. "So don't shoot him."

Sheriff O'Brien burst through the damaged front swinging doors with gun in hand. He looked to Ty and Elihu and then knelt to inspect the body of the Lordsburg outlaw.

Ty moved his gaze to Seth, who was on the floor against the wall. Seth held his broken arm and peered blankly forward in apparent shock. Ty retrieved Seth's gun off the floor and turned to look back out the window. He saw Hamilton kneel before Jess, his hat off in prayer. Ty turned to Elihu and motioned outside. "Jess."

Taking in Ty's manner and tone, Elihu quickly holstered his gun and dashed toward the doors. He burst through them in full gallop toward Hamilton and Jess. Hamilton rose and stepped back as Elihu fell to the ground in front of his best friend, pulling him up in his arms.

"Jess!"

"I am deeply sorry, Elihu," Hamilton said.

Elihu sobbed. Hamilton looked up as Ty stepped through the saloon's window frame.

"Oh my God!" Elihu cried out. "Jess!"

Hamilton peered at Ty, remembering their many past battles, the inevitable death that would accompany such battles, the friends they had lost, and how they had depended on one another through it all. Ty peered back at him, and Hamilton took this as him remembering the same.

"Oh my God!" cried out Elihu again.

Hamilton stepped away.

Ty moved into the street, gazing after Hamilton. His eyes caught something across the street on the opposite corner. In his sight, Audrey Stephenson, a pretty woman of thirty-three years, watched him from the boardwalk. When she caught his eye, she quickly moved on.

"Audrey?" Ty said to himself.

As the woman was moving away, he caught up to her, leaping onto the boardwalk some feet behind her. "Audrey," he called to her.

She stopped, closed her eyes momentarily, and slowly turned to face him. "Hello, Ty."

He stepped closer. They looked at each other for a few moments.

"I . . . I didn't know this is where you made your home," he said finally.

She nodded. "I opened a dress shop," she said, pointing down the street to its location. "I had heard the opportunities were good here." After a pause, she added, "Well, I need to be going. I—"

"I've missed you."

". . . have a son," she finished saying, taken aback at his words. "And he's waiting for me. He's ten now and looks just like you." She looked to the Acme Saloon and added, "I always wondered if things had changed—if things were different with you."

"I'm not the man I was, or at least who you knew me to be."

"I *knew* you to be a good man, Ty. It's just . . . the 'everything else' that came with it." After a moment, she added, "I see now you're standing with the law. Sheriff O'Brien is a good man. Are you going to be in town long?"

"Leaving in the morning."

Obviously struggling, she managed to say, "Well, the next time you're not leaving in the morning, come by and see me and Ryan sometime." She cast her eyes to the saloon once again. "When the odds on tomorrow aren't against you—and me."

Ty started to respond.

"I've got to be going," Audrey said quickly

Ty watched her move away.

———◆———

At the same time, Rachel peered out the window of the moving Southern Pacific on her way to San Antonio. In front of her gaze were endless miles of West Texas. She had sold her Winchester for needed money. Her revolver was secured inside a small handbag she had resting on her lap. The train began to slow and come to a halt.

The male passenger next to her checked his pocket watch. "What could be the problem?" he asked, obviously irritated at the delay. "I have an appointment in San Antonio."

Suddenly, an armed man in his mid-forties entered the car. He wore a leathery, dangerous appearance. His eyes searched the passengers' faces. He met Rachel's eyes and moved determinedly her way, looking unwaveringly at her. She quickly moved to pull her Navy Colt. As she withdrew it, he put a strong hand on her arm, preventing her from bringing it to bear.

The male passenger next to Rachel recoiled, dropping his pocket watch.

"Texas Ranger, Mrs. Donovan," said the man gripping her arm. "No need for alarm."

She held firm to the gun.

"My name is Thurlow Weed. I'm a friend of your father."

At this, Rachel relaxed her stance and manner.

He released her arm. "The description he gave me of you and that Colt of yours was on the mark."

She dropped her gaze to the gun and pushed it back inside the handbag.

He motioned for her to rise. "If you would come with me."

The male passenger peered at Rachel with wide-eyed alarm as she rose from her seat and was conducted from the passenger car.

Outside the train, two mounted rangers waited, holding two frisky horses. Thurlow and Rachel emerged from the passenger car. As a courtesy, Thurlow assisted Rachel down from the car. He then signaled toward the engineer, and the train lurched forward once again.

Thurlow motioned for her to mount.

Rachel didn't budge—she awaited an explanation.

"It's for your own safety, Mrs. Donovan," he explained. "We expect the men who killed your husband will be at the depot. They know you and your father are coming. They were warned by a man named Seth Garrett, a former employee of your father."

Rachel softened her stand. "And where *is* my father?"

"He's right behind you in El Paso. He and his men will be taking the train tomorrow, and asked that you wait for his arrival." He again motioned for her to mount. "We're to escort you in."

Rachel did as she was asked and swung up onto the saddle.

Thurlow nodded once at her. "I am to ensure your safety until he arrives."

The four spurred east toward San Antonio.

CHAPTER TEN

We Were Fearless Then

With the sun low in the sky, Hamilton, Ty, and Elihu emerged from the Grand Central Hotel. Due to the day's events, everyone who was about the hotel had their eyes on the three men. The Republican campaigners did not accost them this time. The loss of Jess was infused in the men's manner and bearing as they moved toward their horses—Elihu's burden, obviously the most. They had made arrangements with the undertaker. They were going to escort Jess back to Tucson by train, but with alternate arrangements made if they did not return to El Paso by a certain date. They swung up on their mounts. With fatherly concern, Hamilton looked to Elihu momentarily, not for the outward wound on his arm, but for the considerable inward one. Elihu returned the gaze and nodded reassuringly. At this, Hamilton spurred his horse lightly, and Ty and Elihu followed.

They slowly passed through the still-busy streets, making their way to the Levi Burch residence, honoring his dinner invitation.

Before long, a campaign speech was heard up ahead. But it was a dissimilar sound to what they had been hearing all day. Different words were being spoken with an altogether different message. This time is was not Blain or Cleveland being elevated, but rather an alternate candidate's name was being lifted up for consideration by raised voices. A group of suffragettes soon came into their sight. They carried various campaign signs, all declaring, Belva Ann Lockwood for President and Equal Rights Party, which Lockwood represented, and other signs of the same message and intention. The suffragettes' attention belonged to a woman, elevated on a scaffold, who spoke before them. Her gesture and movement were infused with emotion. As the men neared, Hamilton pulled up, leaned on his saddle, and listened. Ty and Elihu did the same. She spoke clearly and eloquently:

. . . .I therefore claim the right to speak for the
unenfranchised women
of the country, and believing as I do that the prejudices
which still exist in the popular mind against women
in public life will soon disappear.

There came exuberant cheering and applause among her supporters.

"Well . . . I'll be," Hamilton said. "That's Victoria Woodhull. The first woman in this country to run for president," he informed them. "It was back in '72. A courageous and daring move," he added admiringly.

"Another politician?" Elihu asked, apparently remembering Hamilton's encounter with campaigners when they first arrived.

"Maybe—but her fight is altogether different. She now speaks for the twice-widowed Mrs. Lockwood, who now carries their standard into this year's presidential election."

"What is it that they want?" Elihu asked.

"Among other things, they are unhappy and frustrated with the other parties' resistance to women's suffrage."

"Suffrage?" Elihu asked, his brow furrowed, apparently unacquainted with the word.

"It means their right to vote, Elihu," he said. "I saw Mrs. Woodhull speak in the nation's capital in '72 when I first got into politics. At that time, she herself was the presidential nominee for the Equal Rights Party." He motioned to a few of her supporters in the crowd who were carrying signs from that year declaring, Victoria Woodhull for President. "I didn't vote for her. She had her own fight. I had mine. The candidate I was passionate about was U.S. Grant, even though he and his army damned near killed me in the war. I just couldn't bring myself to vote for his opponent Horace Greeley."

Woodhull continued speaking:

Let all reformers tear from their political banners
the names of Democrat and Republican, which have
become a stench in the nostrils of all thoughtful people,
and throw to the breeze that more comprehensive
name 'Equal Rights.'

Again, cheering and applause rose up among her supporters.

. . .And let them battle for it stoutly and devotedly,
never faltering until it shall be planted on the dome
of the Capital at Washington in the hands of the Goddess
of Liberty, in whose keeping it may be entrusted for all
future ages. This is our destiny!

"Just give ear to her," Hamilton said with admiration over the cheering and applause. "A bold woman, Elihu, with fearless language. Full of sound and fury." He then added in thought, "Reminds me of Julia in her day." He glanced to Elihu. "You ought to marry that woman, Elihu. She's a little older than you, but wouldn't she be *somethin'*."

Elihu looked to him and smiled. "Yes sir, I should."

The riders moved on. Woodhull's voice trailed after them. Her words seemed to wrap around them and speak of their own destiny.

. . . .for in the language of Holy Writ,
"The night is far spent,
the day is at hand, let us therefore cast off the darkness
and let us put on the armor of light."

———————

Under the same light of day, a young Texas Ranger conducted Rachel to her hotel in a buggy through the streets
of San Antonio.

"The Menger Hotel is right up here, Mrs. Donovan," he
informed her. "It's located on the Alamo Plaza—the battle-
ground of the Siege of the Alamo. If you're not aware of
the story—" he started to say.

"My father, being from Texas, spoke of it often," Rachel
said, interrupting in a friendly manner. "I've never seen it,
though."

The buggy pulled up in front of the three-story hotel
with wrought-iron balconies. He motioned across the
street. "There she is. That's the Alamo."

She peered at it for a long moment. "There's not much
left of it," she said, dismayed.

With his eyes on it, the Ranger took a breath and nodded. "Just the old stone church and the long barracks. It's
been taken apart piece by piece and sold over the years.
When the army moved out in '77, *businessmen* took over,"
he said with disdain. "They disrespected it. Among other
dishonors, the church was even used as a storehouse by a

French businessman named Honore Grenet, who rented it to hang hog carcasses in its cool, dark interior."

"What can be done?"

"With the fiftieth anniversary coming up, the State of Texas bought the church last year. They will hire a custodian. It's a start. But we need to do more," he added. "You and I are on the very battlefield where those fearless Texians died fighting: Travis—Bowie—Crockett—Esparza," he listed with reverence in his voice. "Fearless men refusing to surrender in the face of overwhelming odds." The Ranger came out of his thoughts and leaped out of the buggy. He moved around the conveyance to assist Rachel down, but she hopped out without his well-intentioned attendance. At this, he tipped his hat with a smile and they moved toward the entrance.

They entered and stepped through the stained-glass-roofed Victorian lobby, making their way to the front desk.

"I'm to be outside your door for the duration, Mrs. Donovan—until your father arrives," the young man told her.

"Thank you, but that will not be necessary. There is no need to worry, I assure you."

Now at the front desk, he turned to her. "Orders. Sorry, ma'am."

Rachel nodded. "I understand." After a moment, she said, "It's been a long journey. Would you object if I stepped over to the lavatory for a moment?"

"No ma'am. I will be here registering you and will await your return."

Rachel looked inquiringly at the clerk who was now before them and had overheard.

"Around the corner to your left, ma'am," he said as he spun the hotel register around for the Texas Ranger to sign.

Rachel came around the corner and moved down the hall. She looked around for an escape and spotted a maid exiting a room up ahead. "Excuse me—I hate to be an annoyance," she said as she approached the woman. "But I have a relentless admirer out front that I would like to elude. Is there a back exit I could use?"

———•———

All were seated in the Burch's dining room with food and drink before them. The table remained set for six in honor of Jess.

In an amiable manner, Levi turned to Ty and Elihu. "I suppose Hamilton's told you he and I go way back in the horse business."

Elihu nodded.

Levi's eyes then settled on Ty. "What business are you in, Mr. Spooner?"

"Currently, I'm the proprietor of a cantina in Nogales, Mexico."

Levi nodded. "Very good—a man of property and business."

Feeling his liquor, Hamilton spoke up. "Like *hell!*"

At this sudden outburst, Sarah, Levi's wife, looked to Hamilton with apparent disbelief.

"Pardon me, Sarah," he said apologetically, and turned his eyes back to Levi. "Mr. Spooner is just attempting to keep the conversation polite so as not to offend anyone. Could say he was in the 'horse' business, himself. Mr. Spooner's Christian name is Tyson. This is Ty Spooner, Levi. You've heard me speak of him in the past."

"Oh . . . yes," Levi responded, somewhat taken aback. "I do remember."

"I don't understand," Sarah said.

"Spooner here was a most notorious outlaw, Sarah," Hamilton informed her. "Wanted dead or alive," he added, a little too loud. "As governor, I had my name on that particular proclamation. Worded it myself," he added, with a smile and a nod of pride to Sarah. With the effect on her visible, he added, "But prior to all that, we served in the Texas Rangers together."

"Oh?" Sarah responded, obviously surprised.

Hamilton nodded. "That's where he learned he could shoot straighter than most and was quicker at it. After his service, he decided his future would best be spent on the other side of law and order." He leaned over to Sarah and added with emphasis, "I did my best to *hang 'im.*"

"Hamilton!" Sarah exclaimed.

Ty rose from the table. "Ma'am, I will step outside, for the last thing I want to do is displease you after you have served such a first-rate meal."

Sarah turned her gaze to Ty. "Mr. Spooner, I know for a fact the Texas Rangers are an exceptional group of men, for

I am sitting next to one," she said, nodding to Hamilton, "despite his behavior this evening—and I count you the same. I am honored to have you at my table."

"Thank you, ma'am," Ty responded. "But if it's all the same, I'd prefer to step outside."

Sarah nodded graciously.

Ty stepped toward the back porch.

Sarah turned wrathful eyes to Hamilton. "Hamilton Pierce! I realize you must not hold to a high opinion of Mr. Spooner, though at one time you counted him a friend and—"

"And," Hamilton said, stepping in front of her runaway anger, "I still count him as one, Sarah," he said, sobering up. "And from our past association, I do hold to a tall opinion of him, or he wouldn't be ridin' with me now." He rose from the table. "But you are, of course, right, Sarah." He raised his glass. "A toast!"

Elihu and Levi raised their glasses.

"To Sarah Burch," Hamilton began. "A lady who has always warmed the homes she's entered with her presence and beauty; warmed the insides of those she has welcomed at her table; and forever warmed the hearts of all who have known her."

There was enthusiastic agreement from the two men.

"Please accept my apologies, Sarah," beseeched Hamilton.

She smiled. "I've been accepting your gracious apologies for years, Hamilton. I'm not going to stop now." She then rose and they with her. "Now that we have that settled, why don't you gentlemen retire to the parlor. I will join you presently." She moved away.

The men retrieved their drinks and started toward the parlor.

"Being called a gentleman is one of those rare treats I enjoy in Sarah's house," Hamilton said. "I plan to savor it along with one of your cigars, Levi"

"And I've got the best cigars in Texas," he responded.

————◆————

With the night having settled in, Rachel, in a newly acquired evening dress, furtively observed The French House from across the street. It was the brothel Tom Braden patronized—information she'd overheard in the Mesilla jail. It was a two-story, well taken care of establishment, and was located on a street known for its abundant and myriad houses of prostitution. In her sight, women of the evening trolled the avenue, searching for trade. She observed a buggy stopping in front. A well-dressed patron exited and hurriedly withdrew inside. She made one last adjustment to her dress—pulling the neckline lower—and moved toward The French House.

Inside, Rachel entered cautiously, taking in everything. The brothel's baroque interior befitted the nature of its commerce. There was a bar on one side with ornate velvet footstools. The atmosphere was lively as men and prostitutes mingled, reclined on couches, or chatted at the bar.

A splendidly dressed woman approached. "Hello, allow me to introduce myself. I'm Nellie Ringo, proprietress of The French House."

"Tessie Darr," Rachel said in introduction, offering a false name. "Very nice to meet you."

"Please join me for a drink, Miss Darr."

She led Rachel over to a secluded end of the bar for privacy. The bartender set down two glasses of white wine, which they retrieved. He stepped away.

"Now, Miss Darr,' Nellie began, leveling her eyes on Rachel, "I'm sure that's not your *real* name."

Rachel smiled. "No, it's not. I made it up."

"If you hadn't given me a false name, I would have suggested one for you," she responded, smiling in return. "Now—what brings you to my establishment?" she asked, taking a sip of wine.

"I lost my husband recently and have no family."

Nellie nodded in apparent understanding. "You, Miss Darr, are looking for work."

———◆———

In the Burch parlor, Hamilton and Levi enjoyed after-dinner cigars and conversation. Elihu was quiet. Distant fireworks filled the dining room window, drawing the men's attention.

"As you can see, everyone is celebrating a Cleveland victory a might early," Levi said. "They don't give Mr. Blaine much of a chance—at least here in Texas."

Sarah entered the parlor. "Texans have never lacked for confidence or courage."

Hamilton cast his eyes downward in thought, and then lifted them to Levi and Sarah. "If you good people will excuse me, I would like to step outside for a moment."

On the back porch, Ty leaned against a post. He observed the celebratory fireworks in the sky that mingled with the noise of distant firecrackers exploding in rapid succession.

Backlit, Hamilton stepped into the doorway, his silhouette filling the frame. Lighting another cigar, he observed Ty for a moment. He, too, listened to the distant fireworks. His eyes followed the rockets streaking through the sky before exploding in pyrotechnic brilliance. "Last time I saw 'fireworks' like that," he began finally, "you and I were in the Texas Brigade entrenched at the Siege of Petersburg holding off Grant's army. His Union guns opened on our Confederate lines on the evening of April 2, 1865." Hamilton shook his head at the memory and stepped onto the porch. "From Appomattox to Hatcher's Run, the bombardment was kept up until 4 a.m. It was a hell of a night for us. The Union assault began at daybreak."

Ty stood unmoving, his eyes to the celebratory sights and sounds in the night sky.

Hamilton took a puff off his cigar and stepped closer. "We were fearless then . . . but I am sure as hell scared now—for Rachel. I dearly love that woman, and she is all Julia and I have left."

Ty lowered his gaze in reaction to his words.

Hamilton paused a moment in thought and said, "I suppose you and I will always have our differences, but I've seen what you're made of right down to your last bullet—when it looked like there would be no more tomorrows—for either of us. The kind of man I need with me right now; the kind I know I can count on when it gets bad."

Hamilton moved to return inside. He paused at the doorway, his silhouette filling the frame once again.

"And I suspect it will," he said, over his shoulder, and withdrew inside.

CHAPTER ELEVEN

Los Diablos Tejanos

In the morning, Hamilton and the others walked their horses back through the El Paso streets now littered with both the campaign debris of electioneering the day before and the remains of last night's celebration. A few prone, overindulged campaigners lay about on the boardwalk in plain sight while others had found sanctuary—either by design or good fortune—which was less visible to those excessively interested in a person's private affairs and personal failings. Sprawled out up ahead was Mr. Turley, the Republican campaigner who had eagerly accosted them on the porch of the Grand Central Hotel the day before. He lay unmoving, mouth open. His top half was in the street, face to the rising sun, and his lower half was in the shade of the boardwalk.

Hamilton pulled up and observed Turley for a moment. "Hey," he called out in a loud voice to see if he could stir him. The man didn't budge.

147

Hamilton furrowed his brow, swung down from his saddle, and approached him. He knelt and looked him over, scrutinizing his condition. He then placed a hand on the man whose top and bottom were reversely orientated to his surroundings and jostled him. "Are you all right, Mr. Turley?" he asked, to see if he could, once again, produce a response.

The target of his inquiry remained still.

"Is he dead?" Elihu asked.

Hamilton angled a look and saw the tip of a liquor bottle that was wedged underneath the man's top half. With some effort, he yanked it out and peered at the empty vessel. "If I was to speculate, I'd say we're seeing a man who sat here last night and finished off this bottle toasting his candidate, James G. Blaine, while celebratory fireworks exploded overhead. Then, after some time, when he neared an unconscious state, he let drop the bottle, rolled over on it, and lay splayed out as you see."

The Republican campaigner snorted and began to awaken. He grimaced against the sun and closed his mouth.

"Other than that, apparently he hasn't been shot or otherwise harmed," Hamilton stated.

Ty shook his head. "I've come across men who can't hold their liquor, but it's been a while since I've seen a man that dead drunk."

The Republican campaigner cleared his throat and focused his eyes on Hamilton, whose image would have been upside down to him.

"We came close to burying you, Mr. Turley," Hamilton said.

Not giving any evidence that his words were sinking in, Turley gathered what saliva he could in his parched mouth and cleared his throat again. "I would be grateful," he began slowly, "for your time to vote for our candidate, the esteemed and venerable James G. Blaine," he finished saying, slurring the words he had repeated so often. "He's a man of integrity. A man of vision—"

"Election Day is over, Mr. Turley," Hamilton said, cutting him off. He then lifted him, swung him around, and sat him on the boardwalk. He retrieved his Blaine for President hat that lay nearby and placed it back on the man's head. "You did a fine job," Hamilton said, then stepped away and remounted his horse.

Turley lifted his eyes to Hamilton. "How'd we do?" he asked, squinting in the sun. "I mean . . . who won?" he clarified, apparently attempting to clear his head.

"Cleveland."

"Oh, dear God!" Turley cried out loudly, abject despair filling his face. He dropped his head into his hands.

The riders moved on.

His anguish and despondency trailed them. "It can't be!" they heard him wail as he wept.

"When he sobers up," Hamilton said, "He'll remember we won't get the election results for days."

Before long, they approached the Southern Pacific depot. Hamilton and Ty dismounted and handed their reins to Elihu, who led their mounts toward the rear of the train to oversee them loaded on a stock car. Hamilton and Ty stepped up onto the platform, joining the other awaiting passengers. With them on the other side of the platform was Tennessee Jane Dancer, the woman passenger in Tucson who had taken such offense at Ty. She stood next to her travel luggage and several bags of purchases—an accumulation from a few days shopping in the big city.

Soon the train approached and came to a stop, the brake system squealing and blowing steam. A few travelers disembarked. Moments later the conductor, who had stepped out onto the platform, checked his watch and called out, "All aboard. All aboard for San Antonio."

While others began the boarding process, Tennessee stood erect and unmoving despite the conductor's clarion notice, plainly waiting for assistance with her baggage. Hamilton noticed and started over to her when Ty, who was nearer, instead stepped over to assist this woman whom he had unknowingly crossed paths with in Tucson. This was unknown to Hamilton, but because of her manner and bearing—the way this dignified young woman presented herself to the world—he decided to watch.

Tennessee's eyes locked on Ty as he moved in her direction. At first grateful, she offered a pleasant smile. She peered at him with curiosity as though she were trying to place this good-looking man who was coming to her aid. Then a flicker of recognition crossed her face—evidently remembering Ty from the ticket line in Tucson where she was horrified by his conduct. She was now equally horrified that he was attempting to assist her. Her eyes grew wide in disbelief and renewed offense with each step he took, the distance between them growing shorter.

"Ma'am," Ty said in greeting as he touched his hat. "If you would allow me." He began to gather her baggage.

"Sir, I do not need *your* assistance," she declared. "And if you continue to accost me I will summon a constable."

At this, Ty swung his eyes to her in surprise and curiosity, taking in her manner and response. "Yes ma'am," he said politely. He promptly dropped her baggage onto the platform with a thud. He smiled once again, tipped his hat another time, and moved to board the train.

Tennessee glared after him with an arrogant distaste.

Having observed the exchange, Hamilton stood amused. He stepped forward to offer his assistance with her bags as an alternative. "May I?"

At his proposal, the young woman breathed a sigh of relief. "Thank you, kind sir," she said, with an engaging smile. "Your assistance is welcome and appreciated."

"My pleasure, ma'am." He gathered her belongings and they boarded the train.

Inside, Tennessee found a seat, and Hamilton stowed her baggage. He tipped his hat and started away toward Ty and Elihu sitting a few rows forward.

"Sir?" she quickly said, calling after him.

Hamilton turned.

She offered another smile. "Would you care to join me? I do so hate traveling alone, and would enjoy good company."

He nodded in acceptance. "As would I. It would be my pleasure." He took a seat next to her, and before long the locomotive whistle blew and the train lurched slowly forward. They were leaving the depot and El Paso behind. She was clearly happy to have a companion for the long journey.

As the West Texas landscape passed before them, Tennessee peered out the window for a moment and then turned to Hamilton. "I am not sure if you realize, but we'll be traveling right through Comanche country," she informed him.

Hamilton nodded politely.

"Or is it Kickapoo?" she asked, correcting herself with a laugh. "Honestly, who would know the difference?"

"When they start shooting arrows at you, you learn the difference pretty darn quick," he said good-naturedly.

She smiled at his response. "Oh, please don't jest." She extended her hand. "I'm Mrs. Tennessee Jane Dancer. Please call me Tennessee."

He returned her smile. "Hamilton Pierce," he responded in introduction. "Pleased to make your acquaintance, Tennessee."

She breathed a sigh of relief. "Well, it's nice to be seated next to a gentleman." She glanced in Ty's direction. "You never know on excursions such as this just who you might have the misfortune of encountering."

"Yes ma'am," he responded in a strong voice meant to reach Ty's ears. "Men of the worst kind."

Clearly overhearing, Ty turned an irritated gaze out the window, then leaned back and tipped his hat down to rest.

Evidently comfortable with her companionship for this journey, soon Tennessee closed her eyes, leaned her head against the window, and went to sleep.

Hours into their journey, her cheek found rest on Hamilton's shoulder. A jolt of the train awakened her. She took stock of her position and straightened in her seat. Embarrassment filled her eyes and manner. "I'm—I'm terribly sorry to inconvenience you like that, Mr. Pierce," she said apologetically.

Hamilton shook his head politely. "No inconvenience, Tennessee." He saw her embarrassment and wanted to alleviate it. "As a matter of fact, you were of great assistance to me."

She looked at him with curiosity.

Hamilton continued. "I was—" he began, then cut his words short. He gave a furtive look to those seated near them as if what he was about to share with her was of a great personal nature. He then leaned in close to her as if preparing to part with this private information that was of great secret to him. Curious, Tennessee leaned in, giving ear to him. He spoke in a low voice that only she could hear. "I was born lop-sided, and—to my great mortification—I tend to fall out of my seat. Your cheek balanced me and kept me from great humiliation."

Somewhere in the middle of his story, she began to smile. "That's absurd," she said inoffensively as he finished, clearly appreciating his levity. "Mr. Pierce, you are a delight. I do so hope your business in San Antonio, whatever it may be, is a success."

"I'm staking my life on it."

She returned a laugh and said, "You mustn't jest so." She then took on a manner and deportment as serious as the message she was about to deliver. "Texas is an untamed country, and you will need knowledge of the gun."

"I do my best to sidestep trouble, Tennessee."

"My husband can shoot cans off a fence at thirty paces," she announced to him with obvious pride. "I do hope you brought some protection with you. This country is swollen with men of abominable character."

To ease her concern, Hamilton opened his coat pocket to reveal a concealed revolver.

She angled for a better look, her eyes growing wide. "Oh, my . . . is it loaded?"

"Yes, it is, Tennessee," he said, then concealed it once again. He added softly, "I was thinking it might not be much help if it wasn't—that is, if I happened to find myself in an unpleasant situation."

The young woman sat back and came to an apparent conclusion. "Mr. Pierce, you and my husband have a lot in common." She cast her eyes down and said with humility, "I have been told I am a handsome woman—"

"That you are, Tennessee. No easier words have been said."

"Thank you, Mr. Pierce," she responded with a smile, obviously pleased to receive a compliment and that he had noticed. "And as such," she continued, "I am at the mercy of rogue men. When I travel alone, I rely on individuals such as yourself—men of high character."

"Well, Tennessee, you can rest assured that I—as a man who has knowledge of the gun," he began, then raised his voice for Ty's benefit, "will shoot any man of low morals who accosts you on your journey."

Elihu turned to Ty and smiled—apparently aware that Ty was being made sport of.

Tennessee beamed gratefully and turned to gaze out the window, once again, at the boundless West Texas landscape. "Some people might recount to you that it was those unsavory Texas Rangers that settled this majestic land. No indeed! We could do with fewer of *those* men. My husband, Orville P. Dancer, of the San Antonio Loan and Trust, declared to me, it is men like himself that are making Texas a more safe and civilized place for people like you and me."

Hamilton acknowledged politely.

Tennessee went on. "As I am sure you are mindful, their bank provides the funds for the growing businesses in this uncivilized country." She then added with obvious concern,

"They're suffering the terrible peril of non-repayment." She gathered a fury within her. "No, not those Texas Rangers!" she said in an accusing tone. "Glorified killers is all!"

Hamilton took a moment, remembering his days on the frontier and then responded in a gentle instructive tone. "Well maybe, Tennessee, those rangers were surrounded by desperate individuals trying to kill not only them but also the worthy citizens of Texas, like yourself. And to endure they had to be just a little bit meaner than those trying to kill them."

"Oh, no, Mr. Pierce. I can tell that you have been led astray by some fast-talking men. You need to be more guarded with whom you give credence."

"You are right, Tennessee. I will do that in the future."

"Why, those Texas Rangers are made up of men of the most infamous character. In the Mexican War they were known as *Los Diablos Tejanos*! Are you informed of what that means?"

Hamilton feigned ignorance. "No. I'm sorry, I'm not, Tennessee."

"It means—The Texas Devils!" she said in a hush.

Just then, the train began to slow and come to a halt. Tennessee glanced out to the empty vastness outside the window. "We are in the middle of nowhere," she declared. "What could be the matter?" she asked with concern.

As before, an armed Thurlow Weed entered the passenger car. His eyes found Hamilton, and he moved determinedly his way.

This expected, Ty and Elihu rose and gathered their things. Hamilton met Thurlow's gaze as he approached.

Tennessee eyes grew wide as the dangerous-looking man grew nearer. "Mr. Pierce?" she said, with concern and growing fear.

Hamilton turned to his new friend reassuringly. He liked this woman. She was a good woman. "No need for alarm, Tennessee."

Off her expression, Thurlow informed her, "Texas Ranger, ma'am," as he came to a stop before them.

"Texas Ranger!" she repeated, obviously jolted and astonished.

"Let's go," Thurlow said to Hamilton.

Tennessee's initial shock turned to defiance for her new friend. "Mr. Pierce, do not let this scourge of Texas ride roughshod over you in such a manner!"

"Hello, Thurlow. Good to see you." Hamilton said, then rose from his seat and gathered his things. Then, with warm eyes, he peered down at Tennessee, who looked up at him in confusion and curiosity. "Tennessee, I was once a Texas Ranger," he said. "And as one, I fought alongside of them. I truly hope such an admission doesn't intrude on our new-found friendship. I consider you quite a lady." He gathered the hand of the now-shocked woman, lightly kissed it, and followed Thurlow, Ty, and Elihu out of the car.

Tennessee, her mouth agape, quickly turned to the window and angled for a better look. Against the infinite landscape were two mounted Texas Rangers. One held the reins of Thurlow's mount.

Elihu led their horses down the ramp of the stock car. The men mounted, and Thurlow signaled to the engineer. The train lurched slowly forward.

Inside by the window, Tennessee peered out in wonder at the slowly passing scene. With her eyes on Hamilton, she watched as he and the others spur their horses and gallop away. Her eyes reflected an awe. Still somewhat in shock at what just transpired, she turned from the window in evident thought. After a moment, a warm growing smile of admiration for the man she'd just encountered crossed her face.

CHAPTER TWELVE

Opening Night of *The Rivals*

A hard fist struck Thurlow, knocking him to the floor of the San Antonio Ranger office. Hamilton stood over him. Checking his jaw, Thurlow peered up at him. "Now hold on, Hamilton," he protested, attempting to calm the situation. "The Ranger I assigned to her didn't know she would try to flee. Hell, he was there to protect her!" He picked himself up off the floor.

"I want her found!" Hamilton demanded, adding incredulously, "Again!"

"Well . . ." responded Thurlow, "we'll most likely find her in one of the whore houses—"

Another hard right from Hamilton sent Thurlow to the floor once again.

Ty looked to Hamilton with a bemused smile.

"Damn it, Hamilton! Touchy as ever," Thurlow declared. "Now, if you'd just let me finish," he implored, attempting to shake off the effects. From Thurlow's manner, one could tell he was aware that there was no animosity in Hamilton's assault, and that he was just concerned for his daughter and was getting it out of his system. From the floor, Thurlow started again. "I was going to say, we hear talk that Braden likes to patronize a few of the parlor houses while he's in town."

Hamilton calmed and cast his eyes aside in thought. Following Thurlow's thinking, he realized where he was going with this and said, "Could be Rachel knows that, too."

Thurlow nodded, checking his jaw again. "At least, it's a possibility. He favorites a place called The French House. We can start there." He took a moment and then asked, "*Now* can I get up?"

———◆———

The evening's clientele were gathering inside The French House. Rachel moved about the reception room making polite conversation. Without being self-evident, she was hunting a particular man, which she disguised as courtesy. She made introductions with all the patrons in her search for Tom Braden.

She took notice of a group of men on a plush couch in a corner and approached them. With them were the escorts they had selected for this particular evening. They had made their choices for the night. As she grew near, the men paused their celebratory drinking and laughing and turned their eyes to the beautiful woman who had the obvious intent to speak with them.

"Hello, I'm Tessie Darr," she said, introducing herself with a smile.

The men returned introductions with great courtesy.

"I apologize," Rachel responded, not hearing the name she was seeking. "I didn't realize all of you men had found company," she said, feigning ignorance. She then started to step away.

"Miss Darr, we sure don't mind squeezing you in," one of the men offered.

"You gentlemen enjoy yourselves," she answered. "I think I'll find a couch where the count isn't so even," she said, smiling, and retreated.

Before long, she noticed a patron alone at the bar, his eyes on his drink in front of him. She observed him for a moment, and moved his way.

"Hello, I'm Tessie," she said, moving in next to him with a smile.

The man turned his eyes and thoughts from his glass to her and that's where they stayed. "Well, hello," he said finally, his tone revealing his spirits were now lifted.

"I couldn't help notice you were without company this evening," Rachel began. "Is it by choice? Or is it just early and the only selection you're interested in at present is your brand of liquor?"

He turned bodily in her direction and offered a hand in introduction. "William Henry Sedley, at your service."

She took his hand. "Your service or mine?" she responded with a smile, playing the part.

The man laughed lasciviously.

Having learned what she needed, Rachel looked to the bartender and motioned. "Pour him another."

At this, the man smiled broadly, evidently thinking things were really going his way this evening.

"It's on me, Mr. Sedley. I'll be back later. Excuse me," she said and stepped away, disappointed again.

Let down, the patron looked back after her. "But—"

Rachel moved on to another assemblage of men and women on another ornate couch and made small talk. With the same result, she excused herself and stepped away. Suddenly, her breath was taken away as she was aggressively forced up against the wall by a strong man. His hands were already around her waist. He smiled with a lustful hunger and moved in close.

"Excuse me for startling you," he said. "You're an impressive woman, and I couldn't help noticing you move about as if you were looking for someone."

Rachel made an attempt to free herself from his grip, but it held firm.

Exuding charm, he continued, "I, on the other hand, believe I have located who I am looking for, and I hope you feel the same."

Rachel stopped resisting, and met his eyes. "We'll just have to see, won't we?" she said, recovering from his vigorous introduction. "I'm Tessie Darr. And you are?"

Later, outside The French House, Hamilton, Ty, Elihu, and Thurlow observed from across the street. With Thurlow was the young Texas Ranger Rachel had eluded. The men were dressed in nice clothes, their weapons concealed. On the lamppost behind Hamilton, a playbill promoted the opening night of the play *The Rivals* at the Metropolitan Theater.

Hamilton looked to Thurlow. "Ty and I will check here."

Thurlow nodded. "I'll check another place just down the street I heard Braden frequents," he said, and he and the other Ranger moved off.

Hamilton and Ty crossed the street toward The French House. Elihu stayed behind.

The two men entered and paused momentarily inside the foyer. Their eyes quickly searched the establishment for Rachel while sizing up the patrons. Not waiting for a formal invitation, they moved into the interior and peered about.

Nellie Ringo had noticed, and after a moment stepped over to the unfamiliar, purposeful-looking men. "Gentlemen, you're new to The French House," she announced, getting their attention. "I'm Nellie Ringo, proprietress. How can I assist you?"

Not wanting to identify himself for all to hear, Hamilton did not reciprocate with an introduction. He retrieved the tintype of Rachel at her wedding from his coat pocket and extended it to her. "Miss Ringo, have you seen this woman?"

Obviously wary now of these men and their purpose, she glanced at the photograph in his hand, the friendliness gone from her eyes. "Why?" she responded with crispness. Behind her, the bartender pulled a double-barrel shotgun and placed it on the bar in a manner to be noticed by Hamilton and Ty.

"Any trouble, Miss Ringo?" the bartender asked.

With this obvious warning and threat backing her up, Nellie Ringo peered at the men, awaiting an answer to her question.

Hamilton moved his eyes from the shotgun back to her. "She's my daughter, Miss Ringo," explained Hamilton. "Her name is Rachel Donovan, and her life is in jeopardy."

"Are you Hamilton Pierce?" she asked.

He nodded with curiosity as to how she would know him.

Off his expression, she explained, "I spent some time in Arizona. It's been some years, but I've seen your likeness." Taking the wedding photograph in hand, she glanced back and waved off the bartender, who nodded and went about his duties, though keeping the shotgun visible on the bar. "Is this her husband?" she asked. "She told me she had no family."

"He's deceased. Shot dead by outlaws in the streets of Lordsburg. He was the marshal there," Hamilton explained.

Her eyes met his, obviously taken aback at what he said.

"She's seeking the men responsible," Hamilton added.

At this, Nellie nodded, evidently understanding his worry and the urgency of the situation. "She began working here yesterday," she informed him. "But not by that name. But most of my girls work under a false name. I thought it strange that she refused the entreaties of all customers that were, shall we say, interested in her. I thought she was just taking her time easing into a business she was unfamiliar with." She returned the tintype to Hamilton. "Now I know why."

"Is she here?" he asked with a quickness of manner and concern.

She shook her head. "No. She just left for the Metropolitan Theatre with a good customer of mine. He entertains business associates there."

"Who is this man?"

She hesitated.

"It's urgent, Miss Ringo," Hamilton prodded her, his eyes filled with worry.

She peered at Hamilton for a long moment and then gave in. "Tom Braden."

In the darkness outside, Elihu leaned back against the lit lamppost with the playbill for *The Rivals*. He quickly straightened when he saw Hamilton and Ty hurriedly exit The French House and hail a buggy.

Hamilton called out to him. "The Metropolitan Theatre. Find Thurlow and meet us there."

A buggy pulled up to the theater bearing Rachel and Tom Braden. An eager young attendant approached. Above the front entrance, a banner announced Opening Night.

"You must hurry," the attendant said. "The performance has started."

Braden stepped around and assisted Rachel from the buggy.

The young attendant filled them in on the play's proceedings. "At this point, Lady Lydia Languish has professed her love for Ensign Beverley." And with flare and a mischievous smile he added, "Ahhh, but there is deception. Someone is not who they say they are."

Braden handed the attendant a silver dollar. "Be here immediately afterwards." He looked to Rachel. "The lady and I have . . . plans," he said, with an immodest smile.

"Yes sir!"

To one side of the grand entrance was a large billboard resting on an easel declaring what was seen on the signpost earlier:

OPENING NIGHT!

at

The Metropolitan Theatre!

THE RIVALS

An English comedy by Richard Brinsley Sheridan

As originally acted at Covent-Garden Theatre in 1775

Hamilton and Ty's buggy charged through the streets. Startled citizens sprang out of the way, some yelling after the vehicle with a few well-chosen words after their close calls.

———◆———

Inside the theater lobby, there were murmurings of anticipation from a few groups of enlivened patrons who still had not moved inside the theater proper to take their seats or were seeing to other matters. Tom Braden and Rachel entered and moved toward an ornate staircase, with she holding his arm.

"Tom!" came a call of greeting.

He paused and turned to the voice. "Hello, Frank," he responded in pleasant recognition.

The man approached and extended a hand in greeting. "What brings you to town?" His eyes moved to Rachel. "Or should I say *who* brings you to town?"

"Business brings me to town," Braden responded. "But she is making it enjoyable," he added, looking to Rachel. "Tessie, this is Frank Tanner. We've done business together. Frank, this is Miss Tessie Darr."

She extended her hand, which he took.

"It's a real pleasure, Miss Darr."

"Where are you sitting?" Braden asked.

"Box number eight."

"We're in twelve." Braden informed him as he started away with Rachel. "You and your wife drop by."

He and Rachel proceeded up the grand staircase to the second floor. They moved down the hallway toward their box. The dialogue from the characters in the in-progress play followed them:

THOMAS
Zooks! 'Tis the captain. Is that the lady with him?

FAG
No, no, that is Madam Lucy—my master's mistress's maid. They lodge at that house, but I must go after him to tell him the news.

The two approached Braden's private box. Braden pushed aside the curtains and they stepped inside. In the dim light sat three shadowy men Rachel couldn't quite make out. Braden exchanged nods with them. He retrieved two drinks from a serving tray and offered one to her, which she accepted. He sat her and himself in front.

Glancing rearward to the men she found herself with, Rachel froze momentarily. The one seated nearest her was Juan de La Rosa.

LUCY
Indeed, ma'am, I traversed half the town in search of it...

Here was the man she remembered from that morning in Lordsburg. The face that was seared into her memory as she stood on the boardwalk.

LYDIA LANGUISH
And could not you get The Reward of Constancy?

LUCY
No, indeed, ma'am.

LYDIA LANGUISH
Nor The Fatal Connection?

Juan de La Rosa was laughing and enjoying himself with an outlaw friend of his whom Rachel recognized as one of the men who stood with him that morning. Next to him was a man she did not recognize, probably a local outlaw who had joined them, she thought. Unaware, they paid no heed to her. She turned away, her eyes back on the actors on stage. Her mind raced.

LYDIA LANGUISH
Heigh-ho! Did you inquire for The Delicate Distress?

Audience laughter soon brought Rachel out of her thoughts. Braden turned to her and smiled. Collecting herself, she returned his smile and proceeded to watch the performance.

JULIA
Come, come, Lydia, hope for the best.—
Sir Anthony shall use his interest with Mrs. Malaprop.

LYDIA LANGUISH
But you have not heard the worst.
Unfortunately, I had quarreled with my poor Beverley,
just before my aunt made the discovery, and I have not
seen him since, to make it up.

JULIA
What was his offence?

Outside the theater, the galloping horse and buggy carrying Hamilton and Ty came to a halt. They leapt out. Hamilton quickly gave the driver a few dollars and they hurried past the attendant toward the entrance.

"Sirs, you are late," the young attendant called after them. Filling them in on the play's progress, he told them, "Sir Anthony Absolute has arrived in Bath. A violent quarrel is imminent!"

Hamilton and Ty hurriedly entered the theater. Their eyes searched the lobby. Only a few stragglers of the city's wealthy select persisted in the lobby, apparently more interested in the socializing than the play.

Thurlow and the young Texas Ranger soon followed. As Thurlow advanced, his eyes were fixed on Hamilton and Ty questioningly.

Reading him, Hamilton shook his head.

"Rachel and Braden must be seated," Ty said, informing Thurlow.

Thurlow nodded and walked off with purpose. "I'll find out where."

Inside Braden's private box, Rachel took notice of Juan de La Rosa and the two outlaws getting to their feet.

FAULKLAND
….What grounds for apprehension, did you say?
Heavens! Are there not a thousand? I fear for her
spirits, her health, her life…

Rachel sensed De La Rosa leaning in between her and Braden, so close she could feel his breath. "Tom, if you and your beautiful lady will excuse us," she heard him say, "we'll return shortly with more refreshments."

In the lobby, Hamilton and Ty awaited Thurlow's return. Up the grand staircase, the second-floor entrance to the theater proper opened. Juan de La Rosa and the two outlaws exited and started down the steps toward Hamilton and Ty. Before the door closed, the plays dialogue drifted down to them.

CAPTAIN. ABSOLUTE
He is likewise a rival of mine…

The outlaws descended into the lobby. Juan de La Rosa regarded the imposing men—Hamilton and Ty—as he and his companion passed by on their way to the bar. Unaware of who the others were, none knowing what the others looked like, they all nodded courteously to one another.

In box twelve, Braden looked to Rachel and reached over to take her hand. Playing the part, she turned to him with a smile and let him take it.

FAULKLAND

Well, sir, but you was saying that Miss Melville
has been so exceedingly well—what, then, she has
been merry and gay, I suppose ? Always in spirits, hey?

ACRES

Merry, odds crickets!
She has been the belle and spirit of the company
wherever she has been—so lively and entertaining!
So full of wit and humour!

In the lobby, Thurlow returned. "They're in a private box—number twelve. I've got us in box number two, on the other side of the theatre, just about right across from Braden's. The best I could do."

"I'm taking Spooner and Elihu," Hamilton informed him. "You and your men wait outside." To stave off Thurlow's protests, he explained, "He might make you out. Right now,

my only purpose is to remove my daughter from Braden.
Following that, he's yours to contend with."

Thurlow sighed with acceptance, and he and the young
Texas Ranger moved to leave.

In Braden's box, Rachel dropped her eyes to the hand
that was holding hers.

FAULKLAND

*Hell and the devil! There! There I told you so!
I told you so! Oh! She thrives in my absence!
Dancing! But her whole feelings have been in
opposition with mine...*

On the second floor, Hamilton, Ty, and Elihu moved down
the hall to box number two. They entered and took their seats.

SIR ANTHONY

*Zounds! Sirrah! The lady shall be as ugly as I choose:
she shall have a hump on each shoulder; she shall be as
crooked as the crescent; her one eye shall roll like the
bull's in Cox's Museum...*

Laughter rose from the audience as Hamilton and Ty
looked across to Braden's box.

SIR ANTHONY

...She shall have a skin like a mummy, and the beard of a

Jew—she shall be all this, sirrah!—
Yet I will make you ogle her all day,
and sit up all night to write sonnets to her beauty!

More laughter erupted. Hamilton spotted his daughter. "Rachel . . ." he said softly to himself. His eyes moved to the man sitting by her side.

"I see her, Mr. Pierce," said Elihu, speaking up. "That must be Braden next to her."

CAPTAIN ABSOLUTE
This is reason and moderation indeed!

SIR ANTHONY
None of your sneering, puppy! No grinning, jackanapes!

CAPTAIN ABSOLUTE
Indeed, sir, I never was in a worse humour
for mirth in my life.

"Spooner?" asked Hamilton, inquiring as to his detection of her.

"I see her," he responded. "How are we going to do this?"

Elihu leaned forward. "I can't make out any others. They appear to be alone."

"There could be more," Hamilton countered. He glanced

to Ty. "I'm going to let her know I'm here," he said with resolve. "Then it will be up to her to remove herself from him safely. I don't want any shootin' until she's away from him. Once she's done that, we can protect her." He rose to his feet. "Be ready," he said to both of them, then left with drink in hand. Ty and Elihu began inspecting and preparing their weapons.

CAPTAIN ABSOLUTE
Sir, I hope I know my duty better.

SIR ANTHONY
None of your passion, sir!
None of your violence, if you please!

Ty rested his revolver on his lap.
Hamilton made his way through the hallway to the other side of the theater.

LUCY
What, would you have me tell her a lie?

SIR LUCIUS O'TRIGGER
Ah, then, you baggage! I'll make it a truth presently.

Hamilton approached box number twelve with drink in hand.

LUCY
For shame now! Here is someone coming!

Outside the curtain, Hamilton heard Rachel's voice speak softly in conversation. He paused momentarily. The sound of her voice was impactful. He then took a deliberate breath and determinedly stumbled into the box, making himself appear inebriated. Braden turned and regarded him. Hamilton staggered, sloshing his drink. "Hey!" he said to Braden. "You're in my private box!" he declared, slurring loudly.

FAG
So, so, ma'am! I humbly beg pardon!

"What!" Braden responded in a hushed manner.

Rachel recognized her father's voice. Shocked, she turned, and she and Hamilton locked eyes for a moment.

LUCY
O Lud! Now, Mr. Fag—you flurry one so.

Irritated patrons from the nearby boxes and from down below hushed them.

Beside himself, Braden responded in a low voice. "Get out of here, you drunken fool! You're in the wrong box!"

"Oh, what the hell," Hamilton slurred loudly "You can stay. I don't mind. The more the merrier," he added with a sweep of his hand and a broad drunken smile. He appeared to lose his balance, and his drink spilled once again. "Damn it!" he shouted, and licked the liquor from his hand.

The beseeching from the patrons for quiet from around the theater grew louder.

FAG

....You play false with us, madam...

Hamilton squinted across the theater as if realizing his drunken mistake. "Hey! You're right," he slurred loudly to Braden. "This isn't my box. There's my pal over there," he declared, pointing.

Rachel looked to the box across the theater. She saw Elihu and a man next to him she didn't recognize. She knew that is what her father wanted her to know. She turned her gaze back to Hamilton for a moment, then to Braden. "Tom, please ask him to leave."

Braden rose. "I'll do more than that." He moved toward Hamilton.

Hamilton shoved him away. Stumbling backward, Braden tripped and fell to the floor.

On stage, while still in character and reciting their lines, the actors turned their eyes upward to Braden's private box and Hamilton.

FAG

How! What tastes some people have!—

The actress portraying the character Lucy turned her attention to Braden's box and Hamilton. Breaking character, stepped away from the scene and toward Hamilton. The play halted. "Please, sir," she beseeched. "Have courtesy and civility."

Hamilton leaned over the box balcony and, with overdone gestures, he said, "My humble apologies to the virtuous people of this proud city." He pointed to an obviously married man in the audience—a man of dignified stature, his wife by his side. "Hey! Didn't I see you at The French House?" The couple was horrified. He then turned a drunken gaze to the stage. "And my deepest apologies to the exemplary troupe of men and women in this performance. There will be, forthwith, no further—" he said, not getting a chance to finish, as he was grabbed by his coat collar and jerked away from the balcony.

Rachel watched as Hamilton threw a few drunken, wild punches at Braden, purposely missing, and then feign tripping and falling to the floor. Braden angrily took hold of his arm, got him to his feet, and ushered him out.

Rachel's concerned eyes stayed on her father as he went through the curtains.

Outside Braden's box, Juan de La Rosa and the two outlaws returned with a tray of drinks just as Hamilton was shoved through the curtains, stumbling into the hallway. Braden followed.

"Miserable drunk blundered into the wrong box," Braden explained, and then returned inside. Unconcerned, the Lordsburg outlaw followed Braden back through the curtains with the tray of drinks. Instinctively, Juan de La Rosa stayed behind, his eyes on Hamilton. The local outlaw stayed with him. De La Rosa peered inquisitively toward Hamilton as he drunkenly made his way back down the hall.

On stage, the actress portraying Lucy again addressed the audience. "The performance shall resume. Thank you for your indulgence."

Inside Braden's box, the Lordsburg outlaw took his seat with a drink in hand. Braden noticed De La Rosa had not entered, and pushed back through the curtains. He followed De La Rosa's eyes to Hamilton moving away down the hall.

"What's the problem, Juan?" he asked as they both observed Hamilton stumble away.

Aware that he was being scrutinized, Hamilton continued the drunken charade as he went.

Juan de La Rosa searched his memory.

LUCY
Sad news, Mr. Fag—A worse rival than Acres!...

With a broad smile, Braden slapped De La Rosa's back. "Come on, Juan. Just a damn drunk." He stepped back through the curtains.

A flicker of recognition crossed De La Rosa's face. "I just saw him in the lobby—and he was sober as a preacher," he said loud enough for Braden to hear.

Inside the box, Braden whirled back around. "What! What the hell is going on here?"

At this, Rachel reached into her handbag and took hold of her Navy Colt revolver.

FAG
Never fear! Never fear!

De La Rosa and the local outlaw began to slowly follow Hamilton down the hall, keeping their distance.

Rachel saw Braden draw his gun and motion to the Lordsburg outlaw, who quickly finished his drink, got to his feet, and drew his gun. They moved to exit. Knowing they were going after her father, Rachel rose from her seat with her Navy Colt revolver in hand, turned, and pulled the hammer back.

SIR ANTHONY
No—I'll die sooner than forgive him! Die, did I say?

"Braden," Rachel said in a firm voice that commanded their attention.

He and the Lordsburg outlaw swung their eyes to her.

"You're not going anywhere," she said. She motioned for

them to drop their guns. They hesitated, then did as they were told.

Braden peered at her with curiosity. "Now why would a whore pull a gun on me?"

Observing from inside box number two, Ty rose with gun in hand. He took aim toward Braden's box across the theater. Elihu did the same.

Down the hallway from Braden's box, De La Rosa and the local horse thief followed Hamilton. A theater manager, obviously agitated, turned the corner, moving determinedly toward Hamilton. "Sir! You must leave at once!" he demanded, and seized Hamilton's arm. "You will not be allowed to disturb the performance again!" He began to forcefully conduct Hamilton away toward the end of the hallway and to an exit.

Juan de La Rosa paused in the hallway and called out, "Hey! Amigo!"

Knowing he was caught, Hamilton drew his revolver and shoved the theater manager through the curtains of a nearby box. The theater manager tumbled in and fell at the feet of a female patron. "My word!" she exclaimed in an exasperated tone. "What now!"

CAPTAIN ABSOLUTE
Sir, you see a penitent before you.

In the hallway, Juan de La Rosa and the local outlaw drew their guns.

SIR ANTHONY
I see an impudent scoundrel before me!

Hamilton fired first. The local outlaw was killed just as De La Rosa fired at Hamilton. The bullet tore into the brocaded wall near Hamilton's head. He took cover around a nearby hallway corner.

Juan de La Rosa ducked into a nearby box number eight. Inside, Frank Tanner, Braden's friend, had risen at the sounds of gunshots.

"What the hell!" Tanner exclaimed.

De La Rosa threw him hard to the floor. His trapped wife screamed.

Inside Braden's box, Rachel held her gun on Braden and the Lordsburg outlaw. Down below there was audience mayhem as patrons rushed for the exits. She briefly cast her eyes to the gunshots down the hall, taking her eyes off Braden and the Lordsburg outlaw.

"Father!" she said with concern.

Braden swiftly drew the Bowie knife he used in Lordsburg and lunged for her. The Lordsburg outlaw followed behind him. Rachel fired, hitting Braden in the chest, propelling him back to the wall. He collapsed to the floor. Before she could react, the Lordsburg outlaw was upon her, his face contorted with anger. Instantly, bullets from Ty and Elihu blasted him back toward the curtains. The continued hail of gunfire propelled him through the curtains and into the hallway, his body impacting against the opposite wall, before sliding to the floor.

Inside the box number eight, De La Rosa snatched Mr. Tanner's wife to use as cover.

"Unhand my wife!" Tanner protested, as he stepped forward.

De La Rosa pistol-whipped him into unconscious, then fired at Ty and Elihu across the theater in box number two.

Elihu was hit in his gun arm, spinning him back against the wall. He moved his gun to his left hand. Ty took quick stock of Elihu and their situation. "Can't get a clear shot. I'm going to Pierce. You cover us from over here."

In pain, Elihu nodded. "Yes sir."

Outside Braden's private box, the bullet-riddled Lordsburg outlaw lay mortally wounded on the floor. He slowly raised himself, resting on one arm. He cocked his weapon and raised it to shoot back through the curtains at Rachel.

Hamilton fired twice, killing him. He reloaded his gun.

Inside his private box, Braden was on the floor, propped up against the wall, bleeding from his chest wound. Rachel had her Navy Colt on him.

"Who the hell *are* you?" he asked, his breath shallow.

"Mrs. Matthew Donovan ... of Lordsburg," she responded coldly.

Astonished, Braden stared at her.

"If you survive your wound," she continued, "I am going to be there when you hang."

He cast his eyes downward in resignation.

Inside box eight, De La Rosa assessed his situation while reloading his gun. His eyes wide with apparent panic, he again grabbed Tanner's wife for cover, preparing to flee. "I'm getting out of here!" he said forcefully. She screamed and fainted, falling limp to the floor next to her pistol-whipped husband, who was slowly coming to. De La Rosa cried out in anger and frustration. He positioned himself next to the curtains, preparing to flee. He took several deliberate breaths, gritting his teeth, and gathering courage. He then let out a guttural yell and dashed through the curtains and fled down the hallway, turning and firing wildly in Hamilton's direction to cover his retreat.

Calmly, Hamilton stepped out from around the corner, his body braced against the wall, and took careful aim at the fleeing De La Rosa. Just as he did, the pistol-whipped Mr. Tanner stumbled out of his box into the line of fire, preventing Hamilton from pulling the trigger. Hamilton stepped fully into the hall.

"Get down!" Hamilton shouted as he pushed him to safety.

At that moment, at the end of the hall, De La Rosa spun around and fired, striking Hamilton in the upper chest. Hamilton fell against the wall and sank to the floor.

De La Rosa escaped through the exit and down a stairwell.

In the lobby there was pandemonium. Patrons were fleeing into the streets. In their panicked flight, they knocked over the easel and billboard announcing the opening night of *The Rivals*. De La Rosa, his gun in his coat, emerged with the escaping theatergoers.

Mr. Tanner got to his feet. With a hand on the wall, he gathered his balance and went back through the curtains of his box. He emerged with his unsteady wife, his hand gripping her arm. They stepped past Hamilton, moving around the corner just as Ty quickly approached. Ty knelt before Hamilton and regarded him and his injury.

"Find Rachel . . ." Hamilton managed to say painfully.

Ty nodded and hurried to Braden's box.

Outside the Metropolitan Theatre, De La Rosa passed by an overwhelmed Thurlow Weed and his Texas Rangers, who were scanning the fleeing crowd. Not knowing whom they should be looking for, they scrutinized the eyes and manner of the men moving past them.

Ty hurriedly pushed through the curtains of box number twelve. Rachel swung her Colt on him. He quickly threw up his hands. "Rachel, I'm a friend of your father," he said. She recognized him as the man seated next to Elihu and lowered her gun. She hurried past Ty and out of the box.

She ran to her father. Elihu was attending to him with his good arm. She dropped to her knees before Hamilton.

"Father!" she said, her voice filled with worry.

Hamilton's eyes lit up. "Oh, thank God—you are all right!" he said, pushing the words past the pain.

She brushed his hair back. "Thanks to you—thanks to you."

Ty approached behind Rachel. He was carrying the out-laws' weapons he had gathered inside and outside of Braden's box. As he neared, he threw the guns and Bowie knife into a private box, which was now empty of patrons, and stood over Rachel's shoulder.

Rachel looked inquiringly at Elihu and his wound.

"I'm all right, Miss Rachel," he responded off her expression, and motioned to Hamilton. "And so is he—I just know it. The doctor has been summoned."

"Thank you, Elihu." She turned her gaze back to her father. "Yes, you'll be fine. You'll be just fine," she said reassuringly." The events began to gather in her mind, as did her tears. "It's all my fault," she said finally.

"The *hell* it is," he responded in weak breath. "I'm damn proud of you, Rachel."

Thurlow moved in with the Texas Ranger Rachel had escaped from earlier. "Sorry, Hamilton, we missed him."

"It was Juan de La Rosa," Rachel said. "Braden's back there in box number twelve," she said, motioning. The young Texas Ranger moved quickly toward Braden's private box. He paused for a moment to regard the dead Lordsburg outlaw who lay outside, and then pushed through the curtains.

"Then he'll be riding hard for the border," Hamilton concluded, struggling to find breath for the words. "If I were him, I'd go west to San Felipe del Rio following the railroad tracks. He'll pick up friends in the railroad towns along the way."

Rachel looked into her father's intense gaze. "I will stay with you."

"Like hell you will!" he said with short breath. He attempted to focus on those around him. "Ty—where's Ty?" he asked, calling him by his first name, which neither had done since they reunited.

Ty knelt. "I'm here."

Hamilton's eyes focused on him. "Ty, you ride with my daughter and get that son of a bitch."

"Didn't figure it any other way, Hamilton," he responded.

Hamilton groaned in pain. "Thurlow will provide you horses," he managed to say.

Thurlow nodded and stepped away, moving back the way he had come to see that this was done.

Distressed, Rachel took her father's hand.

Hamilton moved his eyes to her. "Elihu and I will take care of each other," he said off her concern. He closed his eyes and rested his head back against the wall. "Rachel, meet Ty Spooner. He's been ridin' with me—like we once did." He looked to her once again, and with pained breath added, "Glad you didn't shoot him."

She attempted a smile. "I almost did."

Hamilton laughed painfully, and then took breaths that were coming harder and harder. He let his eyes close once again and squeezed her hand firmly. The doctor arrived and took stock of his wound. She looked to the doctor, her eyes beseeching him.

"I don't know," he said to her. "It's bad."

"Go now," Hamilton said, from underneath closed eyes. "Go!"

She let go of his hand and slowly got to her feet. And with trailing eyes on her father, she let Ty lead her away.

Hamilton opened his eyes and with some effort he watched her as she moved away. "She's going to be all right," he said, his breath almost at a whisper. "She's going to be all right." While the doctor was attending to him, he began to lose consciousness. "It's a fine day, Elihu."

With grief, Elihu replied, "Yes sir."

Hamilton lowered his head and closed his eyes. "A fine day . . ."

CHAPTER THIRTEEN

Mission San José

Rachel and Ty rode determinedly through the Texas country on horses provided by Thurlow. They were leaving San Antonio behind. The night had become mostly cloudy, with the moon breaking through occasionally. Rachel was in her trail clothes. Her mind raced—the events of the night playing over and over. In her saddle scabbard was Hamilton's 1855 Colt revolving shotgun. She looked with contempt at the man riding abreast of her. She suddenly pulled up. "Spooner!" she yelled.

Ty reined in, turning his horse back to her in a manner that indicated this confrontation was not unexpected.

"How much is my father paying you to be such a 'good friend'?" she asked. "What are you getting out of this?"

"Enough."

His curt response sparked her. There was not even the smallest effort at a smokescreen hiding his purpose. No lies, no words of deception accompanying the bald-faced truth of his very presence. At this, she made up her mind and met his truth with her own. "I don't want you riding with me," she said forcefully. "This is where we split up."

"That's up to you, but—"

"You turned your back on my father once before. How do I know you won't do the same to me?"

Unruffled, Ty weathered the storm. "Rachel, your father and I—"

"Where were you back there at that theater when my father needed you most?" she asked. "He could die." The words impacted her. She broke off the assault for a moment, casting her eyes aside in thought. ". . . If he hasn't already."

Ty took her anger and remained silent.

She turned her gaze. For the moment, she had no more fight in her. In her sight, in the distance, cast against the moon breaking through the clouds, was the recognizable outline of an old mission with a cross projecting above the bell tower of the church. With a pained expression of concern, her eyes locked onto the distant silhouette, seemingly drawn to it.

Ty followed her eyes. "Mission San José," he said, identifying it. "Its mission activities officially ended in 1824—the land given to the Indian converts, who were residents there. Lately, it's just been a temporary home to soldiers passing through—or bandits. Visiting priests conduct Sunday services for the locals," he added.

Rachel, her eyes never wavering from the shape and shadow of the old mission across the expanse, said in a distant and soft voice, "But . . . it all wouldn't have happened if it wasn't for me. I'm responsible if my father dies." Coming to this realization, she took a deep breath. "I am to blame." The wind picked up, blowing her hair. She spurred her horse toward the far mission.

Ty observed her for a moment and then followed.

She reined in from a gallop as she approached the imposing eighteenth century mission with its tall ramparts made of gray limestone, measuring 330 feet on a side. She trotted her horse toward the arched entrance on the south side. She turned her gaze to a circular bastion at her right, positioned at the perimeter's southeast corner, where there was once a cannon placement, but had been removed long ago. She trotted her horse through the entry and into the missionary post. She halted. Spread out in front of her was the mission grounds dotted by mesquite trees. Ringing the compound were the doors to the Indian quarters, which were built into the mission's thick defensive walls. Across the grounds, on the north side, was the church with bell tower. Her eyes came to rest on the stone cross resting on top she had seen in the distance. The wind began to blow more consistently. The clouds moved across the moon once again. With a light spur she urged her horse forward and moved deeper into the interior, staying close to the east wall. She passed the Indian accommodations one by one and their outdoor fire pits made of stone. She could make out the remnants of the blacksmith shop. As she neared the other end, she turned west and moved along the two-story *convento*, the missionaries' quarters. She peered up to the walled second floor where the priests resided. The first floor was open and decorated with stone arch entries and was used as a refectory, storeroom, and kitchen.

She next came upon the connected church. As she passed by the south side, moving toward the entrance on the west side, she took notice of the church's single window. It was nearly seven feet tall and not far off the ground and was embraced by an ornate sculpture of architectural design. She angled her horse closer. She could see that the baroque carving was framed by two columns. Extending outward were four carved arches with limestone leaves embroidered across the stone. An ornamental wrought-iron grate covered the glass.

Coming around front of the church, she dismounted and noticed a small cemetery not twenty steps from the sanctuary's double doors. Beyond the graveyard on the northwest corner of the mission was a granary. She turned her gaze back to the two-story church and paused to take in the whole of it. She moved toward the entrance with its religious portal carving above the aged wooden ingress.

From underneath the arched stone gateway, Ty watched her move inside the chapel. He looked skyward at the gathering weather, and then walked his horse across the grounds, passing by and underneath the mesquites and where there had once been a corral.

Rachel took a few steps inside the church. She was halted by the soft glow of lit candles, revealing rubble covering the floor and pews. To her left was the mostly collapsed north wall, and above her was a missing roof— all of which she had been unable to see from the outside. The nave of the church was rectangular and about a hundred feet deep with rows of pews on each side. The collapsed vaulted roof lay everywhere, its remains and rubble covering the floor and benches. Rachel looked around in disbelief at the ruins and then peered up to the now-visible bell tower and the night sky with its gathering clouds.

Ty dismounted near Rachel's horse and began to unsaddle. Apparently engaged by an inward thought, he paused and looked toward the sanctuary doors she had passed through.

Rachel took a deliberate breath and moved slowly down the aisle, which had been purposely cleared by human hands. Elaborate stone carvings on the walls that had survived the calamity decorated the damaged interior. Hanging in front of the chapel was a crucified Jesus overlooking all and still giving comfort to the troubled who might enter. Rachel's eyes locked on this image of the Lord as she moved down the central approach. Reserved for the clergy and altar, she paused before the chancel, which was separated from the body of the church by two stone steps.

She then knelt before Him. Her eyes glistening, she bowed her head in silent prayer.

Ty stood on the outside of the chapel entrance, holding the door partially open. He observed her for a moment, then quietly closed the age-old chapel entry. He moved to Rachel's horse and began to unsaddle. A priest approached Ty, and they conversed.

Inside, Rachel rose from her kneeling position and moved back down the aisle. She was met by Ty entering carrying two bedrolls, his Winchester, and her father's Colt revolving shotgun. He tossed a bedroll to her.

She stood unmoving. "I meant what I said," she told him firmly.

"Didn't figure it any other way."

Rachel motioned to the lit candles about her. "Someone is here."

Ty nodded. "One of the visiting priests I mentioned. I spoke with him. He saw us enter the church. He's taken refuge in the priests' quarters for the night." He lifted his eyes to the night sky. "A storm is coming," he informed her as he handed her the shotgun. "I've sheltered the horses. It's best we do the same."

'There's no *roof*," she said in an unfriendly manner, as if he what he had said was nonsensical.

Ty nodded as he glanced upward. "Storm in '68 brought it down," he explained, "along with the north wall you see there." He stepped past her. "Follow me," he said, moving down the aisle toward the front of the sanctuary.

Defiant and still unmoving, she angled a look back over her shoulder at him.

Apparently realizing Rachel wasn't following him, he paused and looked back at her. "The sacristy," he said with a nod toward double doors to the right of the chancel. "Its roof *is* still intact."

"How would you know?" she shot back, her hostile manner unchanged.

"I've spent a night or two here before."

"Were you one of the outlaws you were referring to who used this place of worship as a hideout?" she asked derisively.

"Your father and I used it was a stopover a few times when we were rangers," he came back, then continued on, angling toward the doors in the corner.

Her eyes stayed on him as he entered the sacristy, then she brought her gaze forward once again. A light rain began to fall about her and on her person. She looked skyward and sighed. Giving in, she adjusted the bedroll under her arm, turned and followed him.

She entered the sacristy, the rain now coming down harder into the nave behind her. She closed the door to the scene and paused to look around at the side room where priests prepared for a service and where vestments and other things used in worship were kept. It had a three-domed ceiling with a large window on the south side and a double-doored exit in the rear that led to the *convento*. On one side of the room, Ty was already rolling out his bedroll.

She tossed her bedroll down on the other side.

After a while, she lay looking up at the ceiling, arms folded, hands behind her head. Her gaze turned to the sound of rain hitting the imposing, seven-foot-tall window. It was up a series of steps, and set four-and-a-half feet above the floor. She could see ornate stonework on the other side of the glass and realized it was the sculptured window she had seen from the outside. A lightning flash filled the windowpane, setting off the decorative metalwork covering the glass.

"It's beautiful," she said quietly, but more to herself than to Ty. She caught herself and glanced to him. "The window, I mean," she explained, but not wanting to be friendly. "I saw the outside sculpture," she added simply, and returned her eyes to the ceiling.

"It's called *La Ventana de Rosa*—the Rose Window."

Her eyes moved to the window once more. "Why?" she asked, her manner standoffish.

"The story goes that a Spanish sculptor named Pedro Huizar carved it in honor of his sweetheart, Rosa. It was to be a monument to her. When it was done, he sent for Rosa, but she died in a shipwreck on the voyage here. Remorseful, Huizar refused all other women for the remainder of his days. He also carved that religious portal you saw above the entrance door."

"That's sad," she sighed, listening to the rain on the roof, her voice remote.

"It's also hogwash, according to your father."

She angled a look to him.

"'Meant for people who don't know dung from wild honey,' he said to me one night when we were here."

She offered a weary smile and turned her gaze back to the ceiling. She had heard her father use that particular phrase many times.

"Your father is particular about history, and he informed me that Pedro Huizar was from Mexico—not Spain—and was known to have married twice and fathered three children. He did work here, but his talents lay with carpentry, not sculpture. And he didn't step foot inside this mission until twenty years after the Rose Window was finished."

Rachel shook her head in amazement. "Then the window's name is a mystery, huh?"

"Your father said the best explanation he heard was that the window was named after Saint Rosa of Lima, the first saint of the New World."

The storm raged outside.

After a long pause, she said, "I want to know how much my father is paying you."

Ty did not respond.

Determined to get an answer, she turned her eyes in his direction and began again. "I *said*, I—"

"A pardon," he answered her, before she could finish a second time. "And twenty-five percent ownership of the Pierce Ranch."

Her breath was audibly taken away. Deeply affected, she

returned her eyes to the ceiling. "Twenty-five percent . . ." she repeated to herself in disbelief. After a moment, she added in thought and realization, "I am costing my father twenty-five percent of everything he has worked for all his life." She then turned her thoughts to the man she found herself with. Anger welled within her. "That's quite a haul for a man like *you*," she said derisively. "Better than stealing horses and robbing trains, huh?" she followed flippantly, not expecting an answer. "What are you going to do with it all?"

"That's none of your business," he responded matter-of-factly.

She shook her head with disdain and turned her eyes to the sacristy ceiling once again—to the sound of rain against the secure and time-tested roof. Before long, she closed her eyes, exhausted, and fell asleep.

The morning light illuminated the Rose Window. Jostled awake, Rachel opened her eyes to a smiling priest standing over her.

"Good morning," he said to her in a heavy Spanish accent.

Rachel slowly rose. "Good morning, Padre." Gathering her thoughts, she looked momentarily to the empty space where Ty had slept. She got to her feet. "The man I was with—when did he leave?"

The priest looked confused and repeated the few words of English he knew. "Good morning," he said again. He gestured toward the door.

Understanding his communication dilemma, she smiled.

From her person she handed him some paper money. "*Para los niños, Padre*," she explained.

"*Gracias, senorita! Gracias!*" he responded, smiling broadly.

Rachel gathered her bedroll and shotgun.

She opened the doors and emerged into the sanctuary. Through the missing roof, the indirect sunlight fell starkly upon the ruins. She could better see the destruction within the nave. Through the mostly crumbled north chapel wall, she beheld the nearby north perimeter rampart of the mission only a dozen steps away, beyond which lay the hydraulic gristmill, where the mission's residents had made flour. She looked once more to the image of the Lord hanging over the altar and then moved back down the aisle toward the church entrance. She pushed open the aged door and stepped outside into the bright sunlight. Squinting, she was halted by the sight before her. Ty was mounted, and he held the reins of her horse standing next to his.

"I think your father is right," he said, speaking up. "I'll bet we'll pick up his trail alongside the railroad tracks."

Rachel's eyes moved from her already-saddled horse to him. "How did you know I had changed my mind?"

"I didn't."

She regarded him momentarily. "I am thinking we stand a better chance together," she said, explaining her change of mind. "But the second it's over," she added firmly, "you and I go our separate ways. You understand?"

"Didn't figure it any other way."

CHAPTER FOURTEEN

The Frio by way of Hondo

They rode west through the wide expanse, alongside the rails. The previous night's rain had erased any tracks, or if not completely removed them, left them unreadable as to their freshness. Mid-morning, the ground firmed up. They had moved beyond the range of last night's storm. Ty kept his eyes to the ground and quickly picked up a fresh trail.

Under the blue sky, Rachel took in the landscape and the flora of the Texas Hill Country. Some of the plant life she had never seen before. Scattered about were various cacti unknown to her, like the Texas prickly pear and the hard-to-see horse-crippler cactus with its large, stiff spines, growing only a few inches above the soil—a hazard to a quick-stepping horse. Intermingled in the panorama were the myriad of colors from the fall blooms of the wildflowers, like the vibrant blue of the fall aster or the Texas green-eyes with its yellow flowers and green center or eye. After a while, she turned her gaze to the telegraph line that ran together with the tracks. She had noticed it was still intact. She glanced to Ty. "Why hasn't he cut the telegraph line?"

"He would if he could, I'm thinking," came the response. "But he's on a stolen horse and doesn't have a line cutter, most likely."

"Why would he be on a stolen horse?"

"He wouldn't have gone back to the livery to pick up his own," he explained. "He wouldn't have taken the chance. I'm sure he just jumped on the first horse he could find." After a moment, he added, "I wish he *would* cut the line. That way I'd know for sure it's his trail I'm following and not some employee from the railroad checking the tracks looking for a washout."

———

By midafternoon, they were walking their horses into a small but growing town. Rachel looked about, taking in the budding community. People were immersed in their various tasks and errands. The sounds of hammering and sawing on this street, and those nearby, greeted them. In their sight, men transported lumber in wagons while others put planks in place on the framework of new construction.

Rachel took notice of the various businesses already established and those being assembled. "Hondo," she said, reading a word that repeated itself among those enterprises with hanging signage and others whose names were baptized with paint directly upon the facades.

Ty nodded. "Another railroad town recently sprung up," he concluded. He angled his horse over to the dry goods merchant, and she followed. "You check the train depot," he said, as he dismounted and tied off.

"You think he might have taken the train from here?" she asked doubtfully.

"No," he said, turning back to her. "By now Thurlow has telegraphed ahead to the train depots with the description you gave him. Check to see if they are in receipt of it and if they've seen him. I'm thinkin' De La Rosa got in here ahead of the marshal being informed." He turned and moved toward the merchant entrance. "Let's see if I'm right."

Rachel nodded with understanding as Ty stepped up onto the boardwalk. She turned the reins and started to move away. "Leave your horse here," she heard him say. She looked over her shoulder to see Ty standing in the doorway of the dry goods store, his eyes on her.

"I don't want to be holding supplies waiting for you to return," he said and then stepped into the establishment.

She watched him disappear inside. Somewhat embarrassed that she hadn't thought of that herself, she turned the horse to go back.

Ty approached the owner behind the counter. "Need provisions for two to San Felipe del Rio. Only what we can carry in saddle bags."

The owner nodded. "Changed its name last year, though. It's now just Del Rio. The residents of the town requested a post office, so the name was changed to avoid confusion with San Felipe de Austin."

"Fine then—to Del Rio."

The store owner began gathering items. "Since it's been awhile since you've been in the area, you'll need to know that Uvalde and Brackettville lie between here and Del Rio. You can, of course, pick up supplies there. But you're smart, you never know."

Ty nodded in appreciation of the information he was being given. Then he inquired, "A man might have rode in ahead me. He would've been riding hard and looking for provisions, too."

The owner nodded as he placed items on the counter in front of Ty. "Early this morning," he informed him. "He was wearing nice clothes that looked like he'd rode through rain and mud, and had a thick layer of dust stuck to that dried mud. I'd say he was ridin' a borrowed or stolen horse." He shook his head in memory. "I've never seen a man so ill-fitted to a horse and saddle. I didn't ask him any questions, though. He didn't look like a man for talkin'. I sold him trail clothes and provisions." He then moved his eyes to the front window and pointed. "He walked across the street and bought a Henry rifle out of the gun store. He was soon gone—he didn't wait around long."

———————

Rachel strode over to the Southern Pacific depot. She stepped up onto the platform and approached the ticket window. The clerk, who had stepped back from the window to attend to routine duties, glanced up to the sound of approaching boots and spurs. His eyes widened, obviously taken aback at the sight of this good-looking woman in dusty trail clothes. He snapped to attention and manned the window with an eagerness. "Yes ma'am, how may the Southern Pacific be of service to you today?"

"I'm seeking information."

"Oh?"

"Have you seen a man this morning who is of Spanish descent. Six feet—lean. He would have been traveling alone."

The clerk shook his head. "Nobody by that description, since I arrived. So far, it's been a slow day—only a couple of families heading west to Del Rio."

"Perhaps you received a message concerning this man."

"What's his name?" he asked pleasantly, apparently happy to continue engaging the good-looking woman. "Perhaps he bought a ticket before I came on duty. As it is, I work sixteen hours a day, the night operator only taking eight."

"De La Rosa. But he's known to go by others."

"Oh, yes," the clerk said, the name triggering a memory. "Our night operator received his name and description from the Texas Ranger office in San Antonio. We get these now and then. I found it waiting for me this morning. After I oversaw the early train departure, I walked it over to the marshal's office. He told me to keep an eye out for this man."

She lowered her eyes and nodded in acceptance as though the information just imparted wasn't of the best kind.

"Evidently that's not the news you wanted to hear. I'm very sorry I couldn't be of more assistance."

She lifted her eyes to the man who, by his tone and manner, had evident interest in her. "On the contrary, you've been very helpful," she responded, then offered a smile and moved away.

He angled his head out the window and called after, "I would have handled it differently than the night operator and got it to the marshal post haste. But I can only work so many hours a day," he said, as a last minute plea to win her favor. "If I see this man, I can let you know before I tell the marshal," he offered, hoping to get a response.

She did not reply and continued on, going back the way she had come.

Disappointed at her lack of response, the clerk observed her moving away, the footfalls of her boots and the rowels clicking on wood planks were distinct to the general quiet of the emerging prairie town. She then stepped off the platform and disappeared around the corner, out of sight.

His eyes lingered in her direction—evidently not detecting the sound of a softer-soled shoe approaching him from the other direction.

"Sir," said the well-dressed man now at the window, attempting to get the distracted clerk's attention.

The clerk snapped his eyes to the impatient man. "Yes sir, how may the Southern Pacific be of service to you today?"

Outside the dry goods store, Ty was filling their saddle bags with supplies when Rachel returned. He finished and looked to her questioningly.

"You're right. Thurlow's message was received last night. But the marshal had it placed on his desk sometime this morning by an overworked depot employee."

Ty took this in and nodded with acceptance. "Due to its human component, he's outrunning the telegraph—at least for now. It'll be different in Uvalde."

———————

That night, a few hours outside of Hondo, they sat before a fire underneath a Uvalde big tooth maple with its reddish autumn leaves. Rachel was silent underneath the star-filled sky. She leaned back on her saddle, staring into the flames. Ty gathered wood and added it to the fire. "Spooner . . ." she began. Her tone with him was no longer contentious, her manner no longer combative. She had accepted her situation and was going to learn more about this man with her. "Considering what my father is offering you, I'm figuring he's gambling you'll get killed, so he won't have to square with you."

"That did cross my mind."

Her thoughts were far away. "He spoke of you quite often when I was a small child. Not so much later when you turned outlaw. He said many times if he had caught you, he would have hung you."

"I was lucky."

"I heard reluctance in his words, though. I'm thinking he didn't try so hard."

Ty remained silent

She lifted her eyes to him. "Mother had this picture of the two of you, and a third man, armed to the teeth and heading off to fight for the South." She returned her gaze to the fire. "Still does, I believe. Best of friends, looking so proud. You would have thought you three owned the world."

"The illusions of youth."

"Who was that third man? My father had told me at one time, but it was long ago."

"Nate Farmer. Hamilton and me grew up with him in Gonzales. He was killed at Cold Harbor in '64. It was Lee's last victory. A few days later we were digging trenches at Petersburg, where we stayed for the next nine months to just before the surrender." He then sighed and added, "Nate almost made it to the end of that damn war."

"Mother would sometimes speak of the brutality of it. She endured as much as my father." The fire crackled in the cool night. "Turning outlaw, you turned your back on her as much as my father and everything you believed in—Why?"

"A man makes mistakes in his life—some worse than others." He then leaned back against his saddle and tipped his hat over his eyes to rest.

"My father kept most things about you from me, but as young girl I secretly saw in his desk a picture of you with a newborn child. Was that child yours?"

"No. And before you ask, I don't have a wife, neither," he said from underneath his hat. "At least, not anymore. She was killed in a Comanche raid outside of Fredericksburg many years ago."

At this, she took her eyes off the flames and placed them squarely on him for a moment. She then returned her thoughts and gaze to the fire. "Spooner?" she asked, not yet through with the conversation.

No answer.

"Spooner?" she asked again, a little louder. "You didn't answer my question back at the old mission."

He took a deliberate breath. "That tree over to your right is a pepperwood."

She glanced over. "Yeah, so?"

"It's also known as a toothache tree or tingle tongue. Chewing on its leaves causes a numbness of the mouth, teeth, and tongue. Used for medicinal purposes, mostly. But it has other benefits too—makes it hard to talk. I can pull a few leaves for ya."

"What are you going to do with twenty-five percent of my father's ranch?" Rachel persisted. "It will make you a prosperous man."

Ty tipped his hat up to observe her momentarily, then back. He proceeded to answer her question with the energy and feeling of someone relating a dream they've held for a long time, and delivered in a way an observer might think he was giving her the answer she expected. "Head to Sioux City," he declared. "Buy myself some fancy clothes— gentlemen's clothes with a hat to match. Get myself a place of my own and a fancy lady. Always wanted a Sioux City woman on my arm," he stated. Then he added, "Maybe get two. That would be *somethin'*."

She shook her head with disdain at such a goal. She was repulsed and offended at the way her father's hard-earned money would be consumed. She pulled her blanket up. "Didn't figure it any other way with a man like you."

———◆———

Rachel awoke to Ty moving about the camp, saddling the horses. Not yet sunup, the early morning light beyond the horizon softened the night sky. She threw off her blanket and got to her feet.

"We've got a long ride. Let's get some breakfast," Ty said.

He pulled their supplies from the saddle bags, and they took a seat on the ground. They dined on dried beef, dried fruit, and sourdough biscuits, and washed it down with the water from their canteens.

"If I get the chance," Ty said, finishing up, "I'll shoot one of those black-tailed jackrabbits I've been catchin' sight of." He got to his feet. "They're good eatin'. And more nutritious than that dried meat," he added as he moved toward his horse.

Rachel took a last swig from her canteen and rose.

They mounted up and spurred their horses, riding abreast.

———————

Under the noonday sun, they splashed across the Sabinal River with the railroad bridge in sight in the background. Once across, their horses got traction on the far bank, climbed out, and continued on.

As they rode, Rachel's gaze returned to the landscape.

"Christmas cholla," she heard Ty say. She turned to see him pointing to a cactus with vibrant red fruits arranged up and down the green stems of the cactus.

"It has its winter colors out," he commented. "It got its name 'cause it looks like a decorated Christmas tree." After a moment, he added, "It was nice to look at when you found yourself out here around the holiday chasing down outlaws or Indians."

It was not long before they heard the approach of the Southern Pacific, its chuffing coming up behind them in the distance. Once it was upon them, it blew its whistle in greeting as it passed.

"How long do you think before that train catches up with De La Rosa?" Rachel mused.

"He's no longer following the tracks."

"What?" she responded, dismayed. "We're not following his trail?"

"He turned south a ways back. I reasoned he did it as a precaution—to throw any pursuers off his trail, off his real intention—Uvalde," he explained. "We'll pick up his trail again there. He has friends there, more than likely."

She halted her horse. "You don't know that," she shot back. "We should have turned south with him."

He turned his horse back to her.

"Why didn't you tell me?" she asked, her voice and manner irritated.

"Because I didn't feel like arguing with someone who didn't know any better," he responded firmly. "As I said before, your father's right, he's heading for Del Rio at the border. We just need to get there in time to keep him from crossing into Mexico."

She took a breath and nodded with understanding. "Will we?" she asked after a moment, her manner softened.

"He'll lose time riding a wide loop into Uvalde. I think we have a good chance."

He turned his horse and spurred. She quickly followed and caught up.

212

———◆———

Around midday, Ty pulled up, apparently seeing something. In the near distance a black-tailed jackrabbit, spooked by their nearby presence, leaped from its hideout and scurried across the landscape. Ty quickly dropped from his saddle with his Winchester in hand, took a few steps, dropped to his knees, aimed, and fired.

The black-tailed jackrabbit dropped.

"Start a fire," he said, with his eyes to where the rabbit fell.

Soon, Rachel looked up from the budding fire she was making grow to see Ty walking back carrying the rabbit by its hind feet. A short distance away, he plopped it down and began to skin it.

It wasn't long before the meat was over the fire. Rachel settled back to watch it cook. After a while, she looked out to the distance. In her sight was the goldenball lead tree with its yellow spherical blooms—a tree she recognized from the Tucson area. Nearby was the naked Indian tree, so named for the color of its bark—a tree she had seen in New Mexico travelling with her father. She took a deliberate breath at the memory and then dropped her gaze to wild-flowers just a few feet away. Each had a spiral cluster of small reddish flowers that cascaded down from the top of a stalk. She reached over and plucked one.

"They're called Texas lady's tresses," Ty said. "It's an orchid."

She lifted her eyes to him, her brow furrowed. "Why the name?"

"It's for the way the blossoms curl down the stem," he explained.

She returned her gaze to the flower.

"They appear to be ringlets of hair," he clarified.

"Oh. Yes," she smiled, seeing it now.

"Texas Rangers or lonely cowboys would pick the flower like you did and just stare at it, thinking of the woman they left behind or wished they were with."

"You sure know a lot about what grows out here."

"Just some," he responded. "I spent a lot of time out here in the wild, like that orchid. And I read books. As Texas Rangers, each of us would carry a book or two. We would read them front to back and trade them with other rangers. Considerin' the whole population of rangers, we had a library of books roamin' the Texas backcountry."

Ty leaned over and checked their meal as to its cooking and adjusted it.

He continued. "It's how your father got interested in history. One fateful day, someone passed him *The Last of the Mohicans*. After that, he would trade just about whatever he had to get his hands on a book about history. One time he traded a Ranger his Winchester for *Uncle Tom's Cabin*, which the owner hadn't quite finished, and *Moby Dick*.

"Wasn't his Winchester something he'd be needing?" she asked incredulously.

"He knew he'd win it back, and more, in a poker game," he responded, checking the rabbit a final time. "That's how he got that rare 1855 Colt revolving 12-gauge shotgun you're carryin'." He then pulled their meal off the fire. "It's ready. Let's eat quick and get goin'.

———•———

Hours later, they rode up to another river bank and pulled reins, pausing before the clear current.

"The Frio River," Ty declared, identifying it. "It's Spanish for *cold*. It's spring fed somewhere up river."

"Is it as cold as the name suggests?"

"You'll find out," he said, turning his horse. "Let's find a place to cross," he called back as he spurred away.

Soon they held onto their saddles as their horses swam the river to the other side.

They got to the far bank, both dripping wet from the chest down. They remounted.

Ty turned to Rachel. "Well?"

"Wahoo!" Rachel shouted exuberantly, acknowledging the river's frigid temperature. "The Frio River!" she followed up enthusiastically, and spurred past him.

He smiled as he watched her ride away. "Yah!" he yelled, as he roweled his horse and chased after.

CHAPTER FIFTEEN

Uvalde

With the sun low, Ty and Rachel rode abreast, walking their horses into Uvalde. As they proceeded down its main street, Rachel peered around. The town was alive with the activity of everyday business and social interaction. On a few of the merchant stores you could make out the town's former name, Encina, its lettering still visible under insufficient or time-worn paint. The now-ghostly lettering was a reminder of the town's vulnerable and precarious founding, standing on its new-born, wobbly legs in the harsh days of early Texas. And then, once it was figured to survive its birth, its future assured, it was given a vanity name of a Spanish governor long dead.

Soon, Rachel spotted something up ahead. "There's a cantina," she said, pointing. "That rabbit was a long time ago."

"Let's take care of the horses first."

They trotted up to the stables. Outside, a girl of ten years with long blonde hair had positioned herself atop a fence to overcome her height disadvantage. She was carefully repainting the weathered lettering "Uvalde Livery" to the left side of the entrance. Aware of her potential customers, she quickly finished a letter and hurriedly put the brush down.

"How's business?" Rachel asked with a smile.

The little girl shrugged. "Could be better." She leaped off the fence as Rachel and Ty dismounted and quickly ran up to them. "Hi, I'm Samantha. You can call me Sam. Named after Sam Houston himself!" she said with obvious pride. She then motioned to the livery. "It belongs to my uncle. Want me to tend to your horses?"

"Thank you, Sam," Rachel responded, "but we'll handle that. Just need some feed and a place to stable them for the night."

Sam nodded. "Follow me," she beamed, clearly thankful for the commerce.

Inside the livery, Ty and Rachel trailed Sam, leading their horses into separate stalls.

"We appreciate that very much, Sam," Rachel said. She then handed her a few coins.

Curious, Sam observed as Rachel pulled her shotgun from its scabbard and Ty his Winchester and then leaned them against their stalls. They then removed the saddles and blankets.

Rachel's eyes moved to the young girl. "Seen any other strangers today, Sam?"

Suddenly uncomfortable in manner and voice, Sam answered her. "No . . ."

Rachel and Ty exchanged glances.

"Okay, Sam," Rachel said.

"I'll drop by the sheriff's office when I finish here," Ty said to Rachel.

"I'm going to telegraph Elihu," Rachel responded. "I'll meet you at the cantina." She then knelt and brushed the hair from the young girl's face with a smile and left the livery, shotgun in hand.

Ty's inspected his horse and then stepped over to Rachel's.

After a few moments, Sam spoke up. "You were a Texas Ranger, weren't ya?"

Ty paused to look at the girl momentarily. "Now how did you know that, Sam?"

Again uncomfortable, she dropped her eyes and said nothing. After a moment, she lifted her gaze. "My uncle says you killed many men. And that you are not a good man and that I should stay clear of men like you."

Ty paused, observed her for a moment, then went on with what he was doing.

Just then, the girl's uncle stepped into the livery stable. "Sam! Come on," he commanded. "Your mother's got supper waiting." With this, she dashed out of the livery stable. The uncle and Ty regarded each other for a few seconds, and then the uncle followed after Sam.

Ty finished up and left—inadvertently leaving his Winchester behind, leaning against a stable post.

———◆———

Inside the cantina were several tables of locals enjoying conversation and poker. In a far corner table, Rachel and Ty finished their meals. Ty poured himself another shot of whiskey. "The sheriff was in receipt of Thurlow's message, but he and his deputies haven't seen any sign of him."

Rachel lowered her eyes in thought. "That poor child was frightened."

"I'm guessing De La Rosa picked up a fresh horse and put a scare in the uncle—and the girl—not to tell anyone, before he left."

"He must know he's being followed," she offered.

"At least, he suspects so." He then threw back his shot of whiskey.

It began to rain, and thunder soon followed. Lightning flashed across the darkness.

"Spooner, what if he doesn't ride for Del Rio?" she asked. "What if he figures that's where his pursuers think he's going, and, instead, makes off in another direction?"

"Well, he could swing southwest and try for Eagle Pass. Not much difference in distance, but there ain't nothin' between here and there that I remember. Or, if he hasn't panicked, he could trail southeast along the Nueces to Corpus Christi to throw us off."

"What does your gut tell you?" she asked.

"I think he's panicked. As far as he knows, there's a company of Rangers pursuing him. He'll want to get to the border as quick as he can." He poured another shot.

"So that leaves Del Rio or Eagle Pass. Which one?"

"It still comes up Del Rio—by way of Brackettville," he said. "He's going to follow the telegraph lines. He wants to know who's following him."

"You mean his friends here will inform him?"

Ty nodded. "By the time he gets to Brackettville, there will be a message waiting for him." His gaze then drifted to Hamilton's Colt revolving shotgun leaning against the wall where Rachel put it. "Damn!" He threw back one last swallow of whiskey and quickly rose to his feet.

"Where are you going?"

"To the livery," he said simply, offering nothing further. "I'll meet you at the hotel. It's best we get one room."

"I *realize* that," she said, annoyed. She added, "Two beds, of course."

Ty plunked down a few coins on the table as he moved away. "Unless you like sleepin' on the floor."

He stepped outside the cantina onto the boardwalk. The storm had not let up. He tipped his hat down, braced himself against the weather, and stepped off into the street toward the livery.

Inside the cantina, Rachel pushed her plate away, reached for her shotgun, and left.

At the livery, Sam and her uncle were moving about, carrying out tasks to safeguard and secure the animals against the thunderstorm. As the uncle turned, he was backhanded hard, knocking him against a stall gate. He collapsed to the ground. A vaquero with a hard-bitten exterior loomed over him. He had a holstered gun and a sheathed knife in his belt. His face was contorted with rage.

"Uncle!" cried Sam.

The vaquero swung his gaze to her. "Shut up!" he yelled over a thunderclap. He turned back to the uncle and pulled the knife from its scabbard. "I told you what would happen," he snarled, and stepped closer.

Lightning flashed, illuminating the windows.

Clearly frightened, the uncle peered up to him. "I did not tell him anything."

"I saw you and the girl talking to them," he accused, moving the knife about in his grip. "What did you say?"

A thunderclap followed.

Sam stepped closer to the man. "Nothing!" she said in apparent desperation, her eyes pleading. "I told them nothing, mister!"

The uncle swung concerned eyes to her. "Sam! No!" he cried out.

The vaquero snatched her and held the knife to her throat.

"They brought us their horses, nothing more," said the uncle. "Please let her go."

The vaquero released Sam, shoving her to the ground and away from her uncle. Rolling thunder gathered outside as the rain pounded against the livery planks.

Inside Ty's stall, the Winchester he had forgotten was smoothly and silently lifted.

"If I find out that you're lying," warned the vaquero, "I'll find the girl and—"

"You get near Sam and I'll—" the uncle started to say, his courage obviously stirred by the threat.

The vaquero kicked the uncle across the face. He then whirled around to the sound of a Winchester being cocked.

Ty held the lever-action rifle easy, waist high. He stood firmly and self-assured with it aimed at the man's middle. "Like the man said—he and the girl told me nothing. Now drop the knife and the holster."

The vaquero slowly did as he was told, letting them drop at his feet. His hardened eyes peered at Ty as if sizing him up.

Sam scrambled over to assist her uncle.

"*You've* told me what I need to know—not them," Ty said. He then stepped closer to the man and spoke in a calm easy manner. "Now—you're going to tell me where De La Rosa is heading." Lightning flashed at the windows. Defiant, the vaquero peered at Ty with hate-filled eyes and did not answer. Thunder trailed the lightning. The rain came down harder.

"What horse is he riding?" continued Ty.

"Go to hell," the vaquero sneered.

Ty lowered his Winchester and leaned it against a post. He motioned toward the man's gun on the ground. "Pick it up."

The vaquero's breathing came quicker. His eyes darted about.

The uncle got to his feet, and moved Sam farther away.

"Go ahead. I'll make it fair," Ty offered in a self-assured manner.

The vaquero's fingers reflexively clenched and un-clenched. "Go to hell, *Tejano!*" he spat out finally.

"Thought as much." Ty retrieved the rifle and quickly brought the butt of it hard across the vaquero's face, knocking him to the ground, unconscious.

Wide-eyed, the uncle and Sam gazed at Ty.

"Mister, I am mighty obliged to you," the uncle said.

"Well . . ." said Ty. "You could say we brought it on you." His gaze dropped to the vaquero. "He ain't dead, so you and the sheriff will have to deal with him."

The uncle nodded. "We'll take care of it ourselves. Again, much obliged."

Inside the hotel lobby, Ty entered with a bundle underneath his arm. He wiped off the weather and glanced over at the night clerk. "Donovan room?" he inquired.

"Are you Mr. Spooner?"

Ty nodded.

"Room 204. Up the stairs to your left," the night clerk replied. "Again, I apologize," he added, as his eyes following Ty up the stairs. "It's our only vacancy," he informed him, repeating what he had told Rachel. He then angled his head as he watched Ty move onto the second floor and out of sight. He raised his voice and reiterated, "And, I still will have to charge you double occupancy."

Ty made his way to Room 204. He knocked. "It's me."

Footsteps approached the door from the inside. The door unlatched. The footfalls moved away. He pushed it open and entered.

Inside, Ty found Rachel on the bed claiming ownership.

"One bed," she informed him in case the night clerk had not. "Looks like you're going to have to sleep on the floor," she said, with a satisfied smile.

Rolling thunder came from out the window. The rain battered the window pane. Ty peered about the room. He placed the bundle atop the dresser.

"What are you waitin' on?" she asked, pleased with herself. "The floor ain't gonna get any softer." She then angled a look at what he had put atop the dresser. "That bundle you were carrying doesn't look like a bedroll. Maybe you better go back to the livery and get it—I don't want your complainin' to keep me up all night."

Flashes of lightning accompanied the rain against the window.

"You're right—I won't be sleeping on the bed." Thunder

tailed in behind the light show against the glass. Ty abruptly moved to the bed, grabbed the covers, and rolled Rachel onto the floor on the other side with a thud. "And you ain't either."

In an angry flash, Rachel scrambled to her feet. "What the hell!" she demanded.

Ty then offered his own satisfied smile. "I'm expecting company—maybe." He moved to the window and looked out at the storm. He then pulled the shade and turned to find Rachel still looking hard at him, awaiting further explanation. He moved to the bundle he'd left on the dresser. "I crossed paths with a compadre of De La Rosa's in the livery." He then glanced to her, adding, "One of those friends of his who had been waitin' on us." He returned his gaze to the bundle and untied it. "He got the worst of it. He may or may not pay us a visit."

Finally understanding, Rachel eased her confrontational posture. "You mean—you want him to."

Ty tossed the ponchos onto the bed in front of her. "Either way, we're not going to be here."

———◆———

Later, in an alley next to a merchant's store, the occasional bolt of lightning revealed Ty and Rachel in the darkness and murky rain, squatting up against the store's outside wall in view of their hotel. Rain streamed down from their hats onto their ponchos as they alternated between watching the hotel and take a few moments' rest. They waited.

Through the blueness of the rain and a flash of lightning, Ty looked up to see the vaquero and two other men on horses saunter up to the hotel. Ty shifted his Winchester underneath his poncho. The slight movement alerted Rachel. She peered out from under her hat.

The vaquero and a second man dismounted with shotguns and entered the hotel. The third man pulled a Henry rifle from his saddle and waited. Their horses bucked and kicked some with the sudden flash and crack of lightning.

Ty rose to his feet. As Rachel started to stand, he put a firm hand on her to stay put. He gave her his Winchester and moved into the street.

Inside the hotel, the vaquero and the second man approached room 204. The mark on the vaquero's face from Ty's Winchester was visible. One eye was swollen and mostly closed. They stood for a moment, readying their shotguns. The vaquero kicked in the door. He and the second man rushed into the darkened room.

At the same time, Ty moved determinedly toward the hotel. The flashes of shotgun blasts filled the shade of their second-story room, the sound absorbed by the storm.

Before long, the second man emerged from the hotel first, shaking his head toward the third man. Then he quickly mounted and sheathed his shotgun on the saddle. The vaquero exited, holding his shotgun at his side. On the boardwalk, he stopped as his eyes caught movement down the street. In his sight, Ty's hat and duster composed a shadowy silhouette through the rain as he moved with purpose in their direction. The vaquero peered with curiosity at the murky figure, and then the image came clear. His eyes widened.

"You men looking for me?" asked Ty.

"*Tejano!*" said the vaquero, obviously surprised and fearful. He raised his shotgun.

Ty quickly drew his .44 caliber revolver from his holster and fired twice, blasting the vaquero back against the exterior of the hotel as the now-dying man pulled the shotgun's trigger. The bright discharge blew the second man off his horse and onto the muddy street, splashing into a puddle. He cried out as he writhed in pain.

The sudden bedlam kicked up the horse of the third man, who desperately tried to wield his Henry rifle in the direction of Ty. He fired wildly.

Ty quickly fired two more times, shooting him out of the saddle and into the gutter. A current of water flowed around him. He tried to rise, and then fell back—dead.

Ty straightaway leveled his revolver on the second man lying in the street, whose breathing and movement soon stopped. Ty holstered his gun and inspected the bodies, removing anything of value. Over his shoulder, Rachel approached in the short distance with the Winchester. Ty unsentimentally hoisted the second man up by his trousers and dumped him into the gutter next to the third man, out of the street and out of the way. Ty then stepped up onto the boardwalk. Rachel followed. He paused to look momentarily at the vaquero who sat lifeless against the exterior, his one eye staring blankly upward. They moved inside.

The night clerk, his face bloodied, stood before them awkwardly holding his revolver. "Oh, dear Lord!" he exclaimed, his voice shaky. "They said they were friends of yours. I didn't believe them, but I had no choice. It was you or me."

Ty and Rachel removed their ponchos and shook the wetness from their hats.

"You let the sheriff know it was self-defense," Ty told the clerk.

"Yes sir, I will. I certainly will. They had no call to do what they did to your room—uh, the hotel's room."

Ty moved up the stairs. Rachel followed.

Clearly distressed, the clerk put head into hand. "What will the owner say?" he moaned, more to himself than to Ty and Rachel. "Who's going to pay for the damages?"

"The men lying out in the gutter will be obliged to," said Ty, without turning. "I'll leave what money and valuables they had with the sheriff in the morning. There's enough to cover it." He and Rachel moved onto the second floor and out of sight.

Visibly relieved, the night clerk responded, "Thank you. Thank you," he called after them.

As they moved down the hallway, curious occupants peeked out of their rooms as Ty and Rachel passed. Their murmuring followed them as they proceeded to room 204. Ty pushed the broken door open and they entered.

Ty glanced at the obliterated mattress, then to Rachel. "You can have the bed now."

CHAPTER SIXTEEN

Hell Bent *on Hell!*

At sunup the rain had passed. The sky was blue. Outside the telegraph office, Ty waited on his horse. Rachel's horse was next to his. Rachel emerged with the received response from Elihu in her hand. Trying to outrun her emotions, she moved quickly to her horse to mount. She grabbed the reins with one hand and placed the other that held the grasped message atop the saddle. She paused, her eyes downward. Her emotions had caught up with her. After a moment, she lifted her eyes, staring into the saddle. "My father's going to make it," she managed to say finally. "Elihu says he's going to be okay." She then lifted her gaze to Ty, her eyes tearing. "Said he'll be back on the ranch bucking and kicking in no time."

Ty offered a grin. "Didn't figure it any other way."

She gathered herself and mounted. They turned their horses and moved away. They walked their mounts through the street. They passed the cantina and soon the hotel where they had stayed. As if washed away by the rain, no trace of the violence from the previous night remained. The bodies of the three outlaws had been removed. She observed the citizenry moving to and fro in front of the establishment. The hotel's façade projected normalcy once again.

"The undertaker was quick in removing those bodies," Rachel said. "Someone must have woken him up."

"And I bet he got there with all alacrity. It's why I removed anything of value and put it in the hands of the sheriff," Ty explained. "That undertaker was *no doubt* disappointed when he *no doubt* riffled through the pockets of those men—expecting to enrich himself. Those fine gentlemen most times forget that others need to be paid."

They soon approached the livery stable. Rachel spotted Sam and her uncle outside. "Good morning, Sam. Best of luck to you," she called out.

Sam looked to her uncle inquiringly, who smiled and nodded to her. She dashed out to Rachel and Ty carrying a Mason jar—its contents full.

Rachel and Ty pulled reins and stopped, their eyes on the little girl.

"Good morning, Miss Rachel," Sam smiled. "Good morning, mister."

"Mornin', Sam," responded Ty.

With the little girl's eyes still on Ty, she added, "Mister, I was wrong—you are a good man. My uncle says so, too."

232

The uncle moved in behind her. "The man you are after rides a spotted gray. We sold it to him yesterday."

"It has a white marking on the left foreleg," Sam added.

"Much obliged," Ty responded with a nod.

Sam extended the Mason jar with the light-colored contents to Rachel. "This is for you. It is *guajillo* honey," she explained. "It is made here in Uvalde. It is the finest honey in all the world," she added with enthusiasm.

Smiling, Rachel took the jar in hand. She peered at its unique light color.

The uncle explained. "*Guajillo* is a plant native to this area. It is a bee plant. Bees that seek out the *guajillo's* blonde blossoms produce a honey that is light in color and exceptional in flavor—smooth and sweet."

"You can also give it someone who means a lot to you," Sam added. "They will always remember you."

Rachel reached down to take hold of Sam's hand. "Thank you, Sam. Thank you both. She then stowed the jar in her saddle bag.

"I can tell everyone I have a beautiful señorita as a friend," Sam said.

"And I can say I know a young pretty girl named after Sam Houston himself!" she said, with the same enthusiasm as when the small girl first introduced herself. "How many people can say that?" She waved good-bye, and she and Ty moved on.

As they reached the outskirts of town, Rachel looked to Ty, her thoughts on De La Rosa. "He is going to Del Rio by way of Brackettville—just like you thought," she said, with certainty in her voice.

Ty turned his eyes to her, apparently wanting an explanation.

"The telegraph clerk said the lines went down between here and Brackettville this morning. And that yesterday those men sent a message to Brackettville just before you killed them."

Ty nodded.

They dug in their spurs, leaving Uvalde behind them.

———◆———

That night, coming over a hill, Rachel and Ty reined in their horses. In the distance, a town came ominously into view against the darkened sky. Aerial fireworks exploded overtop the town in vivid colors. The sound of scattered ground fireworks followed. Sporadic gunfire could be heard joining in with the celebration.

"Let's slow down and walk them in," Ty said.

"Brackettville?" inquired Rachel, wanting to know what they were seeing.

Ty nodded. "When your father and I were younger we knew it as Las Moras—the name of a nearby spring and the creek it feeds. From that, everyone knew where the town was. Its name was as much a direction as it was identification. As it grew, the founder decided he wanted his name on it for all of Texas to see. Then people unfamiliar with the town had to look on a map to see where it was." He swung his gaze south and pointed. "It began as a supply depot for that fort."

She followed his eyes to see the silhouette of a lantern-lit citadel against the sky in the distance.

"Fort Clark," he said, identifying it. "Its purpose is to help guard the Mexican border and defend against Indian raids from either side of the Rio Grande. There's not so much of that anymore. It was also there to protect the trade route between San Antonio and El Paso that 'Rip' Ford help establish. He rose to captain in the Rangers and recruited Hamilton and me."

"I remember my father speak of him."

"That fort is also where the Buffalo Soldiers are garrisoned."

She turned to him, wanting to know more. "Buffalo Soldiers?" she inquired, having never heard the expression.

"All-black army regiments," he explained. "It was a nickname given by the Comanche."

She turned her gaze back to Brackettville. "The town looks lively enough."

"For now," Ty stated with a detectable sigh. "As we saw, the Southern Pacific tracks dipped south of us on the way here from Uvalde—the town's been bypassed," he added, as if it had a terminal disease. "When your father and I were Rangers, it was the liveliest town in west Texas," he said in apparent memory. "The night life could only be likened to the saloons in Nevada and Colorado during the silver and gold fever. Travelers will dry up now that the railroad went around it."

They soon entered the town, moving slowly down the main street. Sporadic gunfire, fireworks, and celebratory voices infused the night. Rachel and Ty continued past various merchants: Brackettville Feed & Grain, W.S. Stone – Undertaker and Furniture Dealer, and Chris Hill Bootery. The saloons were filled and spirited.

"Let's find a hotel and pick up De La Rosa's trail in the early morning," Ty said. As they were passing a saloon, above which the owner had christened in large letters "Holy Moses," he spotted a man in a sombrero on the boardwalk, backing into the shadows. Ty halted his horse, his eyes fixed on the man.

Rachel did the same.

The man in a sombrero instantly ducked into an alley and disappeared.

"Let's get off the street," Ty warned, and turned his horse toward the Holy Moses. Rachel followed. They dismounted and tethered their horses. A drunken cowboy bolted through the swinging doors of the saloon, firing his revolver in the air in celebration. "Cleveland, by God!" the drunken cowboy yelled. The horses spooked. Ty instantly drew his revolver. The inebriated cowboy was followed by another in the same condition. They stumbled into the middle of the street. "A Democrat is elected! Wahoo!" cried out the other.

"Well . . . the country has a new president," Rachel said in thought. "Grover Cleveland got elected." And then added, "Those men sure had their favorite."

The cowboys shot their guns into the air again, the loud retorts a sharp reply to the surrounding celebratory fireworks.

Ty holstered his gun. "Those men couldn't care less. If the Equal Rights Party had won, they'd be drinkin,' shootin,' and singin' songs to Belva Ann Lockwood," he commented. "Just an excuse to celebrate—as long as it wasn't the Prohibition Party."

More gunfire was heard on a distant street.

"More celebration?" Rachel inquired.

"Maybe."

Ty pulled his Winchester from his saddle, and Rachel drew her father's Colt revolving shotgun. Gunfire splintered the hitching post alongside Ty. His return fire from his Winchester came a split second later toward the dark end of the street where the shots came from. He hustled down the boardwalk. Rachel followed. Keeping to the shadows, they moved down the street.

"More of De La Rosa's men?" she asked. "While he makes a run for Del Rio?"

"This feels different," Ty said. "Maybe we've overtaken him. Or it could be he's just stopped runnin'. He got that telegraph from Uvalde letting him know it was just you and me followin' him. He's not afraid of us."

They continued and paused at a corner to take in the situation. On the next street over, a bottle rocket streaked through the night sky and exploded. The colorful flames and sparks floated slowly down, followed by raised celebratory voices. Ty and Rachel turned down another street, again keeping to the shadows, and advanced warily up the boardwalk to another saloon. Piano music and drunken laughter spilled out. Rachel kept a lookout as Ty peered in over the swinging doors. In his sight was a long mahogany bar and many tables, around which were spirited cowboys and saloon girls. In the corner was a no-talent "ivory thumper" banging away on the piano. Ty's experienced eye and ear recognized the familiar card games of faro, brag, and poker, along with the dice games called high-low, chuck-a-luck, and grand hazard.

He continued cautiously past the saloon, and Rachel followed. Their senses were alert to every movement and sound. They came to an old adobe chapel—the doors open. Inside, several late night parishioners were praying in the candlelit interior, which illuminated Ty and Rachel as they passed by.

Rachel glanced to Ty. "I was for Belva Ann Lockwood," Rachel declared, referring to Ty's earlier comment.

"Didn't figure it any other way."

At a corner, Ty and Rachel quickly crossed the street into the shadows once again. Exploding aerial fireworks overhead briefly illuminated a prostitute plying her wares in the same shadows. Her prospective customer quickly disappeared at the sight of the two armed strangers. As they passed her, Ty paused, reached in his pocket, pulled paper money and held it out for her to take.

"It's all I have," Ty said.

The prostitute peered at him with curiosity.

He extended it closer to her. "Go ahead—take it."

Taken aback, she lowered her eyes to the substantial amount of money he was holding. She slowly reached out to accept. "I—I don't understand . . ."

"If things don't go well tonight, I don't want it to end up in the hands of an undertaker searching my pockets. I'd rather you have it."

She took the money in hand, and Ty and Rachel moved on, with the stunned prostitute looking after them.

With their eyes on the surrounding darkened streets, they soon neared the Hell Bent saloon, whose black-lettered name was in the process of being appended. At the saloon's entrance, a lady from the local women's temperance society was atop a stepladder with paintbrush in hand. A bucket of red paint rested on the platform. Two ladies below were holding firm to the ladder, supporting it, and were peering up at her progress. The determined woman with the paintbrush was in the process of adding a couple of choice crimson-hued words onto the end of the name of the offending establishment, with the idea that the appellation should, instead, read "Hell Bent *on Hell!*" She finished the second 'L' and dipped her paintbrush to begin the exclamation point. Surrounding the three women were several sign-holding ladies from the same movement, who were protecting them from interference by the nearby irked proprietor and a few of his customers who were standing about, scratching their heads—all at a loss as to what to do.

Scanning across the street, Rachel saw a spotted gray horse in front of the Buckhorn Saloon. On its left foreleg was a white marking, just as Sam had described it.

"Spooner!" she said in an urgent but low voice.

Ty spun around.

"It's De La Rosa's horse." She then leapt off the boardwalk, sprinting toward the saloon.

The temperance lady with the red paint added the dot on the exclamation point.

"No! Dammit!" Ty shouted as he started to pursue Rachel.

Gunfire from several guns from the same direction ripped through the darkness, with one bullet finding its mark, clipping Rachel's arm. She fell to the ground, losing the Navy Colt revolver from her waistband.

At the same time, shots splintered a hitching post near Ty. With the gunfire came the cry and quick death of the horse nearest Ty, knocking him over as it toppled.

Rachel scrambled to the cover of a nearby wagon, her Colt revolving shotgun in hand. Several shots kicked up dust around her.

The sign holding temperance ladies, the saloon proprietor, and his customers scattered for cover. The two ladies holding the ladder for their friend, stood firm, their eyes wide with panic.

"Hurry, Prudence!" said one of the ladies holding the ladder.

Prudence dropped the paintbrush and proceeded down the ladder as quick as her Victorian ankle boots could take her. As she neared the ground, the two ladies holding the stepladder apparently felt they had done their duty and let go, quickly scurrying away. The descending lady then leapt to the boardwalk from the last few rungs, which shook the ladder—the paint bucket teetered. More gunfire erupted from down the street as Prudence hurried away, following the others. The bucket of red paint toppled down onto the boardwalk, splattering and spilling across the wooden planks.

Down the street, Juan de La Rosa peered around the corner of the Pioneer Meat Market, an establishment located at a side street corner. He cocked the lever of his newly-acquired Henry rifle from Hondo, smoke rising from the barrel. A local outlaw—the man with the sombrero Ty and Rachel had seen earlier—reloaded his revolver. Another compadre, who wore a vest, kept watch.

Outside the Buckhorn Saloon, Rachel made attempts to retrieve her Navy Colt revolver, recoiling as gunfire kept her at bay. She took stock of her wound. The bullet had torn through the meat of her arm—but it was still usable. She wrapped her wound with a bandanna.

Ty took what cover he could behind the horse's carcass. Another shot hit the dead horse's saddle with a thud. "Rachel!" he called out as to her condition and location.

She started to respond to Ty when several more shots hit close by, forcing her to quickly retreat into a nearby alley with her revolving shotgun in hand.

Juan de La Rosa raised his Henry in Ty's direction once again, but his aim was quickly obstructed by inebriated men emerging from the now-monikered Hell Bent *on Hell!* saloon. Drawn by the gunfire, they were celebrating and shooting their guns, joining in on what they believed was more festivity. "You are lucky, *Tejano.*" De La Rosa called out to Ty.

Rachel turned into the back alley, advancing toward De La Rosa.

Withdrawing from the Pioneer Meat Market, De La Rosa and his two compadres retreated down the side street toward the back alley. Illuminated by moonlight and the incidental lantern, they turned into the alley—moving away from Rachel.

Ty hurriedly crossed the street onto the boardwalk in the direction of the Pioneer Meat Market. Gunfire, fireworks, and celebration persisted throughout the town.

Rachel moved forward cautiously. Making out three moving figures up ahead retreating down the darkened alley, she leaned against an adobe wall and brought her shotgun to bear. As they passed through incidental moonlight, she recognized De La Rosa and fired—missing, the loud retort and barrel fire filling the dark alley.

De La Rosa and his two associates turned and fired in her direction, then hastened away.

She quickly fired twice more. De La Rosa and his men returned fire as they withdrew away from her.

The Brackettville marshal, bearing a 10 gauge cut-down shotgun, hurried into the back alley and confronted De La Rosa. "What's going on here?" he demanded. "You men need to—" Without hesitation, De La Rosa fired twice. The marshal collapsed against a wall, and with a dying reflex pulled both triggers of the black powder gun, firing both barrels into the air, briefly illuminating the back alley as De La Rosa and the local outlaws hurried on. Moments later, the back door to a saloon opened and a floorsweep stepped through the darkened threshold of the backroom carrying a filled bucket. Apparently thinking the gunfire was just celebratory, his manner was unconcerned. As he tossed the contents, he was shot in the stomach by the man with the sombrero. The floorsweep doubled over, dropping the bucket, and then stumbled back into the unlit back entrance of the saloon.

Ty paused at the corner of the Pioneer Meat Market. He listened to the gunfire in front of him. Wanting to bring the fight to himself, he hurried down the street to get in front of the back alley gunfire and Juan De La Rosa.

Rachel came upon the marshal's body. Above her, fireworks streaked through the sky. The polished metal of the six-pointed star pinned on his chest caught the light from the subsequent colorful burst. Remembering the star her husband had worn, she paused momentarily. She retrieved the handgun from his holster to replace the one she had lost. A gunshot from down the alley hit a plank board near her. She returned fire with the revolver until it hit an empty chamber. She tossed it aside and continued with her shotgun in hand.

Ty peered around the corner of a side street. He spotted three moonlit figures crossing from the back alley from right to left, firing at an unseen pursuer behind them. "Rachel," he said to himself, identifying their target. Ty stepped out and fired, killing the local outlaw with the vest. De La Rosa and the man with the sombrero quickly returned fire in Ty's direction and then scrambled away, continuing down the back alley. Ty hurried down the boardwalk to once more get ahead of them.

Rachel paused near the body of the man with the vest. Exploding firecrackers on a nearby street blended with distant celebratory gunfire. She lifted her eyes from the dead man. "Spooner," she said to herself.

Down the back alley, De La Rosa and the man with the sombrero moved through a small corral at the back of an establishment. Skittish at their presence, the horses snorted and the donkeys brayed. De La Rosa paused and peered behind him in Rachel's direction. The two men then moved into a side street to cross. Their eyes caught something down the side street and quickly turned to face it. In their sight, Ty's dark silhouette stood challenging, his image back-lit by the lantern lit main street behind him and distant exploding aerial fireworks. Relaxed, Ty stood with his hand by his holster. The two outlaws quickly retreated at the sight, firing wildly in his direction, and taking cover back behind the corner of the corral. De La Rosa quickly gathered himself and swung his Henry rifle back around the corner in Ty's direction.

The side street was empty.

Behind them, Rachel moved silently into the small corral and quickly took cover among the frightened animals. Seeing De La Rosa and the man with the sombrero, she brought her father's 1855 Colt revolving shotgun to bear. A frightened donkey stalled in front of her, in the line of fire. She lunged forward onto the hay underneath the donkey, aimed the shotgun through the kicking donkey's legs, and pulled the trigger back. At the sound of the cocked hammer, De La Rosa and the other man quickly spun around. They both fired in her direction. De La Rosa then dove headlong back into the side street to escape. Rachel pulled the trigger, the blast catching the man with the sombrero full in the body, the force propelling him back against the corral wall. Blue smoke filled the air, the muzzle fire igniting the straw in front of her. She quickly pulled the trigger back and fired again, the impact hurling the man with the sombrero into the side street and across De La Rosa's prone body. Rachel quickly rolled away as the braying donkey bucked and kicked and bolted away. The fire spread quickly.

De La Rosa lay in the street, his Henry rifle sprawled to one side within reach. He pushed the now-deceased outlaw off him and reached for the rifle. "Nope," came a voice from behind him. He stopped and turned his eyes to see that Ty's dark silhouette had returned, his backlit profile standing some distance away. He took in Ty's image a few moments, his hand retreating from the Henry rifle. He then slowly rose, fully expecting Ty to make use of his advantage.

Rachel got to her feet—her now-empty shotgun in hand. Beyond the growing flames in front of her she could see De La Rosa in the side street rise to face someone unseen. "Spooner," she said to herself, knowingly. Now, she could only watch.

As De La Rosa stood at his full height, his confidence returned. The light from the growing fire played off him.

Behind Ty, fireworks exploded overhead, the colorful flames trailing slowly to the ground. After which the night sky, darkly hued, returned once again.

"*El Diablo Tejano*," said De La Rosa, acknowledging him. "I heard you were coming for me." Ground fireworks were heard from nearby streets. De La Rosa set himself. His hand readied near his holster. He then said with a smile, "I am very good."

"I heard as much," Ty said.

The exploding firecrackers reached rapid-fire crescendo.

De La Rosa swiftly pulled his gun.

Ty drew faster and fired twice.

The outlaw was blown backward, landing hard on the dusty street. He groaned. His eyes wide, they now stared blankly at the night sky.

Clutching her wounded arm, Rachel reached De La Rosa and gazed coldly upon him. Dying, gun in hand, sprawled on the earth, his eyes slowly turned to meet Rachel's. A glimmer of recognition could be seen, his memory apparently reaching back beyond the theater in San Antonio to that that morning when he locked eyes with her as she cradled her dying husband in her lap.

"Lordsburg," he managed to say with weak breath.

Rachel nodded and kicked the gun from his hand.

Juan de La Rosa felt his life seeping away under her gaze. He then closed his eyes and breathed his last.

Rachel continued to look down upon him. "You're a long way from Lordsburg," came Ty's voice from behind her. With a breeze catching her hair, she turned. Still darkly silhouetted against the lantern-lit street behind him, he holstered his gun.

"But it's finished," he said, turning and moving away.

She remembered their agreement as they stood outside the old Mission San José. She observed him in thought as the distant celebratory fireworks and gunfire continued throughout the town.

Ty emerged out of the darkened side street into a lantern-lit main street.

Rachel hurried to catch up to him. "Ty, wait," she called out.

He turned to face her. She stopped a few feet from him. They regarded each other a moment, their respect clear. Townspeople began to gather to put out the fire.

"Ty?" he said, evidently noticing it was the first time she'd used his first name. "And I was just getting used to 'Spooner.'"

"I was pretty rough on you earlier," she acknowledged. She then took a moment and said, "I guess . . . I'm trying to thank you. My father would say that you earned that twenty-five percent. So, look out Sioux City women," she said with a half-smile and upbeat manner. "Here comes Ty Spooner."

"You can tell Hamilton he can keep that twenty-five percent. That's not why I'm here." He turned and started away once again. "And I suspect he knew it."

Taken aback, she hurried forward and grasped his arm. He turned.

"Then why?" she asked. "Why *are* you here?"

He observed her for a moment, then unbuttoned his shirt pocket and removed the daguerreotype Hamilton had delivered to him in Nogales by way of Elihu. He extended it to her.

She took it in hand and peered at it. It showed a younger Ty holding a newborn child. "It's the picture I saw in my father's desk drawer." She then realized the small child was her. She stood in stunned silence for a moment and lifted her eyes to him.

"It was at your christening," he explained. "You're my godchild. I figured you were never told, and I understood why. *You're* the reason I'm here."

Speechless, Rachel lowered her eyes and regarded the photograph again for a few moments . . . and then lifted her eyes to Ty once more.

He continued. "I was looking to make up for a few those 'mistakes' I made in my past."

"Ty," she started slowly, "I consider you family now . . . and you wouldn't be here with me unless my father considered you as such . . . and, well . . . I'm hoping you feel the same way."

A smile crossed his face. "Didn't figure it any other way."

CHAPTER SEVENTEEN

Never Gave Up on Tomorrow

Audrey swept the floor of her El Paso dress shop. Ryan, her ten-year-old son, ran restlessly about her small establishment. He darted in front of her, unsettling and redistributing the pile of dirt she had just gathered with her broom. She paused and shook her head.

"Go play outside, Ryan," she said.

Obeying her, he ran out onto the boardwalk in her view of his mother and stopped as he caught sight of something.

"Momma?" he said, in a manner alerting her.

Curious, she moved toward the door. "What is it, Ryan?"

Audrey emerged onto the boardwalk and shaded her eyes against the morning sun. She was taken aback at what she saw before her. Moving toward her in the short distance down the dusty street was Ty. He had his saddle bag slung over his shoulder. He was not wearing a gun. He paused as he made eye contact. They locked eyes for a few moments. She dropped her broom. "Ty," she said under her breath, then stepped into the street and moved quickly toward him.

They paused a few feet in front of one another.

He casually let drop the saddle bag from his shoulder. He then stepped forward and pulled her in. They embraced for a long moment.

"Odds were against it, but I never gave up on tomorrow . . . for you and me," she said.

Ryan quickly ran up and joined them, standing next to his mother.

Ty dropped his gaze to the young boy. "I've got something for you, Ryan." He knelt and pulled from his saddlebag the Mason jar of honey that was gifted to Rachel and extended it. "This is *guajillo* honey. It was given to me by a good friend who rode with me, and now I'm giving it to you and your mother. It's from Uvalde. We were told by a girl no bigger than you that it's the finest honey in all the world."

Some distance away, Rachel, and a bandaged Hamilton, observed Ty from their stationary buckboard. Rachel had the reins. Elihu was behind them on his mount, his arm in a sling.

Hamilton watched Ty take Audrey's hand, and observed as man, woman, and child move back toward the dress shop as a family. His mind far in the past, Hamilton looked intently at his old friend. In the distance, Ty paused and turned to look at Hamilton. Their history, respect, and friendship reached forward once more—out of the past. They both understood they'd never see each other again. After a moment, Ty moved on.

Rachel observed, too. She then turned her eyes to her father—her love and respect clear.

After a long moment, Hamilton pulled himself out of his thoughts. "Let's go home," he said, his voice full with satisfaction.

She jostled the reins and the buckboard sprang forward. She turned the horse toward the train depot.

Hamilton pulled from his coat pocket the daguerreotype he had sent Ty by way of Elihu. Ty had returned it to him. His eyes stayed on the youthful image of his friend for a moment, and then returned it to his pocket. He filled his lungs with the morning air and looked heavenward, taking stock of the blue sky. "It's a fine day, Rachel—a fine day."

THE END

Made in the USA
San Bernardino, CA
27 December 2017